MY ONE AND ONLY EARL

Forever Yours Series

STACY REID

MY ONE AND ONLY EARL is a work of fiction. While reference might be made to actual historical events or existing locations, the names, characters, places, and incidents are either the product of the author's imagination or are used fictitiously, and any resemblance to actual persons, living or dead, business establishments, events, or locales is entirely coincidental.

All rights reserved. No part of these books may be reproduced in any form by any electronic or mechanical means—except in the case of brief quotations embodied in critical articles or reviews—without written permission.

Edited and Formatted by AuthorsDesigns
Cover Designed by Forever After Romance Design

Copyright © First Edition May 2021

Dusean, always and forever.

FREE OFFER

SIGN UP TO MY NEWSLETTER TO CLAIM YOUR FREE BOOK!

To claim your FREE copy of Wicked Deeds on a Winter Night, a delightful and sensual romp to indulge in your reading addiction, please click here.

Once you've signed up, you'll be among the first to hear about my new releases, read excerpts you won't find anywhere else, and patriciate in subscriber's only giveaways and contest. I send out on dits once a month and on super special occasion I might send twice, and please know you can unsubscribe whenever we no longer zing.

Happy reading!
Stacy Reid

PRAISE FOR NOVELS OF
STACY REID

"**Duchess by Day, Mistress by Night** is a sensual romance with explosive chemistry between this hero and heroine!"—*Fresh Fiction Review*

"From the first page, Stacy Reid will captivate you! Smart, sensual, and stunning, you will not want to miss **Duchess by Day, Mistress by Night**!"—*USA Today bestselling author Christi Caldwell*

"I would recommend **The Duke's Shotgun Wedding** to anyone who enjoys passionate, fast-paced historical romance."—*Night Owl Reviews*

"**Accidentally Compromising the Duke**—Ms. Reid's story of loss, love, laughter and healing is all that I look for when reading romance and deserving of a 5-star review."—*Isha C., Hopeless Romantic*

"**Wicked in His Arms**—Once again Stacy Reid has left me spellbound by her beautifully spun story of romance between two wildly different people."—*Meghan L., LadywithaQuill.com*

"**Wicked in His Arms**—I truly adored this story and while it's very hard to quantify, this book has the hallmarks of the great historical romance novels I have read!"—*KiltsandSwords.com*

"One for the ladies...**Sins of a Duke** is nothing short of a romance lover's blessing!"—*WTF Are You Reading*

"**THE ROYAL CONQUEST** is raw, gritty and powerful, and yet, quite unexpectedly, it is also charming and endearing."—*The Romance Reviews*

OTHER BOOKS BY STACY

Series Boxsets

Forever Yours Series Bundle (Book 1-3)

Forever Yours Series Bundle (Book 4-6)

Forever Yours Series Bundle (Book 7-9)

The Amagarians: Book 1-3

The Kincaids series bundle (Books 1-3)

Sinful Wallflowers series

My Darling Duke

Her Wicked Marquess

Forever Yours series

The Marquess and I

The Duke and I

The Viscount and I

Misadventures with the Duke

When the Earl was Wicked

A Prince of my Own

Sophia and the Duke

The Sins of Viscount Worsley

For the Love of the Earl

Mischief and Mistletoe

A Rogue in the Making

My One and Only Earl

The Kincaids

Taming Elijah

Tempting Bethany

Lawless: Noah Kincaid

Moonlight Magic: Jenny Kincaid

Rebellious Desires series

Duchess by Day, Mistress by Night

The Earl in my Bed

Wedded by Scandal Series

Accidentally Compromising the Duke

Wicked in His Arms

How to Marry a Marquess

When the Earl Met His Match

Scandalous House of Calydon Series

The Duke's Shotgun Wedding

The Irresistible Miss Peppiwell

Sins of a Duke

The Royal Conquest

The Amagarians

Eternal Darkness

Eternal Flames

Eternal Damnation

Eternal Phoenyx

Eternal Promise

Single Titles

Letters to Emily

Wicked Deeds on a Winter Night

The Scandalous Diary of Lily Layton

CHAPTER 1

Lincolnshire

James Alexander Delaney took a deep breath of the cold crisp air into his lungs, a tight band of sorrow clutching at his throat. Everything seemed to be observed through clouds or as if he were swimming underwater at the lake in Derbyshire, and he had opened his eyes in its murky depth.

The heavy rumble of thunder and the rattle of the carriage traveling on the rutted country road was a distant hum in the backdrop of his grief. One of his very best friends, Mr. Richard Ashford, was interred a few hours before. It was by chance James had been notified of the funeral, and though he'd traveled with all haste down from London, he had missed it.

"Two years," James murmured. "My very best friend, but I've not seen you in two years." He wanted to roar his anguish, but he ruthlessly composed himself and quieted the raw emotions raging through his heart. "I am so damned sorry, Richard. So damn sorry."

Glancing at the modest but well-maintained manor in the distance, James wondered if he should traverse inside to see the family. What could he say to them? He had never met Richard's family. He only knew them through amusing and sometimes wry anecdotes. It had been Richard's eldest sister, Poppy, who had surprisingly sent James a letter, which had reached him in London, informing James of Richard's passing.

James alighted from his carriage along the driveway, hoping the trek to the house would aid him in gaining his composure. Thunder rumbled in the distance, and the sky, which had appeared overcast, finally opened with a torrential burst of downpour. Being a man who believed in preparation for all eventualities, he'd taken his umbrella from the carriage. With efficient motions, he opened the large umbrella and held it above his head. A few people who'd been walking sedately toward the manor's entrance burst into hurried movements.

"Lord Kingsley," his valet called, hurrying over to his side. "Will you go inside, Your Lordship? It is raining awfully hard."

Lord Kingsley. There were times it jolted James to be referred to as the Earl of Kingsley despite occupying the role for a little over two years. "No. I am not staying. We'll return to the village's inn and then back to town tomorrow."

His valet's face creased into mild surprise but wisely made no reply.

"I will walk back to the inn. Order the carriage to depart."

"It is raining heavily, my lord!"

"I am aware of that, Timothy."

"Your gloves, my lord. Shall I fetch them from—"

"No." James wanted to feel the bite of the cold against his knuckles, feel the handle of the umbrella in his palm.

His valet looked like he wanted to protest but bowed and scampered away. James did not see the point of going inside the house and invading the family's grief. He was a stranger to them, and now was not the time to introduce himself and explain the connection he had with Richard. James knew the pain they currently endured. He too had suffered a similar misfortune.

His beloved brother, the previous earl, had suffered a stroke some two years ago. The pain of it had cut their family deeply, and James had immersed himself in taking up the mantle his brother had died for—working tirelessly to save their family from penury.

It had consumed him so much he hadn't found the time to visit Richard, and now regret, so much regret sat heavy in his bones. James was the one responsible for his best friend's death. It was James who had been restless and chomping at the bit as the second son, bored with the constant pursuit of debauchery and frivolity, and wanted to forge his own path swathed in honor and glory. And that path had been purchasing a commission. It had been very stupid of him because he'd since learned there was no honor and glory in war and carnage.

Richard had been determined to follow James, and how merry they had been. Laughing and singing raunchy ballads while marching to get their papers. *Jesus.* James raked his fingers through his rain-dampened hair. He had made Captain, but Richard's army career had ended quite prematurely after picking up a ball in his knee. He had returned to his home with an amputated limb and a disheartened spirit.

Richard had not recovered well, and James had not been there for him. Even though they had exchanged letters, and Richard had assured him all was well, James should have made a trip down and seen for himself.

Now I will be forever late to see you one last time, my friend.

How many blows could one endure before crumbling? James shifted the umbrella and lifted his face to the sky, accepting the icy sting of the rain pelting his forehead. *Many. I am now the earl with immeasurable responsibilities. I will bear and shoulder a thousand blows if necessary.*

Heavy grief weighing on his shoulders, holding the umbrella firmly, James made his way over to the small bridge leading from the main estate to the village. There was a private pathway, and he made use of it, walking steadily. The mud sucked at his boots, and the stinging rain blew beneath the shelter of the umbrella and slapped at his face. Yet he did not allow it to bother him. He spied an overflowing brook through the sleeting rain in the distance with some stone benches arranged beside it. There he would sit, watch the swollen brook, and perhaps say a few words to Richard.

If there was an afterlife, perhaps his friend would hear him.

Picking up his pace, a few moments later, James stopped in his tracks. A young lady garbed in a bright green dress sat on one of the stone benches, uncaring of the downpour. Her attire did not indicate a member of the family. Everyone earlier had been swathed in black. She was soaked, and a mass of vibrant black hair clung in limp curls over her forehead, shoulders and back. And the most heartbreaking sounds sawed from her throat.

This grief was intimate and tugged at the aching regret and pain lingering inside James's heart. Feeling as if he violated her privacy, he turned around only to falter. The girl would catch her death should she allow the rain to pummel her so. At the very least, he could offer her shelter under his umbrella. James turned around and walked over to her. Unexpectedly her head snapped up, and he met her wide-eyed stare.

She had the prettiest silver-gray eyes he had ever seen. They were bright and glossy with tears and reminded him of a spark of lightning in the dark. She was younger than he had first assumed, perhaps a lady of about twenty years, and the beauty of her eyes and hair seemed to be the only things remarkable about her. She looked like a little cat on the verge of drowning.

She returned her regard to the large stone protruding from the brook as if his sudden appearance were inconsequential. James understood. This lady had escaped here to be alone. He had chosen to walk in the miserable cold, back to the inn some five miles away, because he wanted to be alone.

James strolled over and sat, much closer than he would have if the situation were different. When the rain disappeared from her, she glanced up at his umbrella. She did not profess any gratitude, but when her eyes, filled with tears and misery, settled on his face, James felt the touch of them deep inside his body. It was irrational and nonsensical to think it, but the sensations were profound and inescapable.

Without speaking, she shifted her eyes back to the brook. James respected her silence and made no effort to speak. He then noted the toad, trying valiantly to fight against the churning water to perch onto the boulder. Each time it found some purchase, it slid back down into the water, perhaps onto another piece of boulder under the surface. A jump was attempted, and once again, the toad was at the bottom. They watched the toad in silence until it was successful in reaching atop the large stone. There it sat, staring out into the lush green forestry of the surrounding, uncaring of the relentless rain.

"Who might you be, sir?" she finally asked, her mouth trembling as if she fought with her tears.

Unexpectedly he noted that said mouth was lushly curved, that she was delightfully plump, and her dress strained at the seams of her décolletage. "Forgive my intrusion," said James, feeling uncomfortable for noticing her sensuality at this moment. "It was not ill-intended. I am James Delaney."

"Mr. James Delaney?"

He hesitated but was reluctant to mention he was now the Earl of Kingsley. Clearly, Richard had not mentioned it to anyone. It felt entirely unnecessary for James to do so; hence he replied, "You seem to know who I am."

"You are Richard's friend that he tells...." Her voice hitched. "*Told* me so much about?"

His heart jerked. Richard had barely answered any of James's letters. "He spoke of me?"

Somber eyes stared at him. "Of course, why wouldn't he? That was the only time he seemed to smile."

James very much doubted he could speak around the emotions clawing up his throat. "Please allow me to ask your name, and how do you know Richard?"

"I am his sister…Miss Poppy Ashford. I sent notice of his death to an address I saw on a letter you franked to him."

"Thank you, Miss Ashford. Your letter arrived at my country home, and the butler sent it to me in London. It took some time, and I was late in arriving for the funeral."

Richard had referred to her as passably pretty with little prospect of a decent marriage but had a most beautiful spirit, kindness, and charm. "Richard spoke of you as well. I recall his efforts to purchase music sheets for you."

"Yes…I love playing the pianoforte…and I am self-taught. He would buy books and music sheets for me. Richard truly spoke of me," she whispered, those eyes glittering with indefinable emotions.

"Yes, *always* with great fondness." Another truth.

A cross between a sob and a chuckle escaped her. "I have it on the highest authority that brothers find sisters too bothersome, or they are too overprotective to speak about their sisters with friends."

James shifted on the stone bench so he could see her expression. "Richard and I were on furlough and heading home. That journey took us through the countryside, which was already in proximity to our respective homes.

Instead of making his way home, Richard continued on, trekking for miles to buy sweets for you. When I groused that we passed quite a few confectionery shops in the villages, he insisted that he visit a specific shop in London. They alone knew how to make chocolate nonpareils, marzipans, and candied pineapple the way you loved them. I daresay you were a beloved sister, not bothersome at all."

Fresh tears sprang to her eyes, and she pressed a hand over her mouth. "I have disappointed him so these last few months. I hurt him dreadfully with my willfulness and contrary nature. I do not think he forgave my stubbornness."

Her voice was a mere whisper, but it resounded with anguish.

"Did he tell you so?" James gently asked.

Her chest lifted on a ragged breath, and James believed the lady entirely unaware that her hand had found his knee and her fingers were clenched tightly onto his trousers.

"Not in those precise words. But he pleaded with me to marry a particular gentleman, and I most adamantly refused! It must have been his fretting over my future that—"

"Utter rubbish," he said softly, yet the impact of his word jarred her.

Miss Ashford visibly flinched, and the eyes that looked up at him were wide and imploring. He knew what she needed, words of affirmation that she had nothing of which to feel guilty. He knew the emotions that tore at her heart—helpless anger, pain, the fear she might not have done enough to save her brother.

An odd sort of kinship tugged at his heart, and James found himself reaching out to lift the wet tendrils of hair from off her forehead and cheeks. At his touch, the pulse at her throat fluttered, and a soft shudder went through her entire body.

"Every man is appointed to die, some way or another. You had nothing to do with Richard's death."

"I—"

He placed a finger over her lips, sealing her words away. "Nothing."

Yet the dark anguish in her eyes did not abate. James lowered his hand. "If you will allow me to pry, how did you disappoint and hurt him?"

She swiped the tears from her cheeks. A useless endeavor for the harsh rain blew beneath the umbrella, spewing droplets on them. "He very much wanted me to marry the vicar of our parish, for it is a respectable position, and I would be provided for."

"And you were opposed to this gentleman?"

"Not at first. He courted me…and I admired his gentle manners and amiable qualities. He…he offered for me, and I accepted. Richard was also pleased with the match. The vicar…" she cleared her throat. "Mr. Rushworth was new to our parish and the occupation, so he had not yet met either of my sisters."

She glanced away from him, her gaze on the churning water of the brook. "At first, I was anxious for him to meet my youngest sister."

James arched a brow. "Why?"

"Men, it seems, cannot help falling in love with her,"

Miss Ashford replied with a shaky laugh. "She is exceptionally beautiful."

"Ah." He had an inkling of where this story might lead.

"Mr. Rushworth met Rebecca and fell violently in love with her. He informed me he could no longer in good conscience remain affianced with me, not when his affections and passions were otherwise engaged. I excused his crying off. Thankfully, it had not been announced. There would be little to no scandal."

James frowned. "Was Richard insisting on the match going through?"

"Mr. Rushworth begged my stepmother and Richard to allow Rebecca to marry him. Of course, my stepmother refused. A beauty like Rebecca can have her pick of any gentleman. Our sister, who recently married a baron, promised Rebecca a season where she could meet eligible beau of society and make a good match. Mr. Rushworth was crushed, and after a few weeks of nursing his wounds, he offered again for me."

"I am not sure whether to be disgusted or to admire his gall."

She gripped his knee even tighter. "I was infuriated, and of course, I refused! To marry a man so inconstant and easily distracted by beauty. I am aware I am passably pretty, and I have little talent to recommend me, but does that mean I should marry in haste and then worry about his roving heart and attraction?"

James's heart jolted. *Passably pretty?* She was not beautiful in the fashionable sense with blonde ringlets, bright blue eyes, and a tall, slender figure. But she was not uncomely. Or quite as unremarkable as he had first assumed. No…with her flushed cheeks and bright eyes, there *was* something remarkable.

Miss Ashford closed her eyes and lifted trembling fingers to her mouth, tears sliding from beneath her lowered lashes. "But Richard *begged* me repeatedly to accept Mr. Rushworth. We had so many arguments. He called me prideful and a silly romantic. The realities of life say I need the protection of a husband, and…and I could not expect to do better than the vicar." Her shoulders shook, and the tears coursed more freely down her cheeks. "He was so disappointed; we barely spoke in his last days."

"Miss Ashford," James began gruffly. "Poppy…"

Her gaze snapped to his at the intimate use of her name. He knew the guilt she felt, and though he did not know her, James wanted to reassure her, wanted her to feel safe and comforted. *Bloody hell.* "From the letter you sent me, the doctors said he was weak and tired toward the end."

"Yes," she said in a trembling breath.

He reached up and pinched her chin, forcing her to hold his gaze when she attempted to look toward the brook. Those lovely eyes flared, but she did not draw away. "That, Poppy, is the only reason you did not speak as often. Now tell me the last words he spoke to you; what were they?"

"I…" her throat worked on a swallow. Water trailed down her face, tracing the hollow of her cheek. "He told me he loved me very much…and wished…and wished he had been able to provide me with a living."

"There," James murmured. "He said nothing about disappointment…nor at any time did he truly try to force you to marry that vicar. He had the power as your older brother, you know. But he did not. He knew the weakness in his body…and what he took the time to tell you was how much he loved you. Always remember that, and it is those words you keep in your heart, nothing else."

She stared at him as if he were a creature sprouted from the muddy earth. It struck him then that perhaps kindness was a rarity in her life. A shudder went through her entire body, her face crumpled, and she flung herself at him, capturing James's shoulder in a fierce hug.

The action surprised him, and he awkwardly patted her back while fighting to hold the umbrella steady. James stayed silent, listening to the harsh, wrenching sobs, thinking they expressed the very sorrow and regret he felt. Her tears belonged to him, and he shamelessly allowed himself the belief they were the tears he shed for his friend.

"You are soaked to the bones," he murmured when she calmed.

"I do not feel the pain of this cold," she whispered in the crook of his neck before releasing him as if she had been burned. Slight color appeared in her cheeks, but she did not glance away from his regard.

James silently held out the umbrella, and she took it without question. Standing quickly, he shrugged from his greatcoat. He took the umbrella from her and held out his coat. "Put this on. You'll catch your death without it, and I suspect nothing I say will urge you to return to the main house."

She stood, and he assisted her as much as he could with one hand to slip on the coat. Miss Ashford gasped. "It is incredibly warm…and smells most pleasant. Thank you."

They sat, and she yawned a few times. Grief was exhausting. And she would feel the full effect of her tears later. James had no notion how long they stayed sitting there, but it must have been at least an hour. She had stopped crying some time ago and leaned back against the stone bench. He did not startle when she slowly pitched forward to jerk herself awake in time.

"You should return home," he said. "You'll land on your face in the mud and grass should you fall asleep here."

"I cannot," she said hoarsely. "I…I just *cannot*, not now. Not until the pain has faded. Not until I stop seeing my brother everywhere I turn."

"You have an awfully long wait then." Months, years, a lifetime, but he did not say anything so maudlin and realistic.

Miss Ashford did not reply, and James said nothing further. A few minutes later, the same thing happened, and once again, she caught herself from pitching off the bench.

"Good sir," she began, pushing a strand of hair behind her ear.

How that startled him. Good was he? Never before had he heard such an appellation used for him. "Yes, Miss Ashford?"

"Might I avail myself the use of your shoulder?"

His heart twisted. How…improper and unexpected. Still, he would never refuse a lady in such need of sleep… and comfort. "You may," he said gently.

And she did with a soft sigh. The feel of her wet head

against his shoulder was an unexpectedly pleasant weight. Her breathing at first was shallow, and after a few minutes, became deep and even. She truly slept. *Astonishing*.

Several minutes passed, the tempest of the rain eased; however, Miss Ashford's head kept slipping from his shoulder, and at least once, she pitched forward. James carefully lowered the umbrella, glancing at the sky. The rain had transformed into an icy drizzle. Ensuring he did not jostle her awake, he set the umbrella aside on the bench beside him. Quickly shifting, he placed one hand below her shoulder and the other around her waist. Then James lifted and placed her on his lap, her buttocks on his thighs, his chest and arm her pillows.

When he leaned forward and picked up the umbrella, her lashes lifted, and Miss Ashford stared at him. There was no fright or fear in her eyes to find herself intimately snuggled in his embrace. Her lids were red, swollen, and appeared very sleepy.

"I was hoping to offer a more comfortable and peaceful sleep," he said gruffly, quite aware of the tips of his ears burning.

"Forgive my boldness and impropriety," she whispered, lifting her face to his. "I thank you for your unmatched kindness. I shall never forget it."

James held himself still when her lips pressed against his jawline. It was the most chaste kiss he had ever received in all his five and twenty years on earth, yet it sent his senses reeling, his heart trembling.

With a deep sigh of contentment, she shifted down, laid her head in the crook of his neck, and fell back into a deep slumber. The trust she placed in him humbled James and sent a strange ache through his heart. It was preposterous *and* scandalous that he had a young lady in his lap, deeply sleeping, exhausted from her outpouring of grief. It was even more ridiculous that he held her snuggled so with one hand holding her securely to his chest and the other hand holding the large umbrella, protecting them from the drizzle that appeared to have no intention of abating.

If anyone came upon them, honor would demand they marry, and that would be impossible. Even with that knowledge, James did not move her from off his lap. He stayed there until the rain stopped, until the sun lowered in the sky, and until the effort to hold himself still so that she was not disturbed became a burning ache.

It mattered to James that she rested. And damn if he would move despite his burning shoulders. A bird screeched in the distance; the wind ruffled the leaves on the trees. Miss Ashford stirred, and her lashes fluttered open. James glanced down at her, and her cheeks flushed a becoming pink. He helped her sit up when she struggled slightly, and she gently rose from off his lap to stand.

"Thank you," she said. "I do not know how to repay your kindness, Mr. Delaney."

He slowly stood. "There is nothing to repay, Miss Ashford. You are the sister of one of my dearest friends."

They stared at each other in silence for several moments. James did not understand why his heart started its slow and almost painful drumbeat. There was something about her unfathomable gaze.

"Perhaps someday we shall meet again, Mr. Delaney."

"I hope that we do, Miss Ashford. Please allow me to walk you home."

She glanced toward the pathway leading to the manor house then back at him. "It is a path I've walked many times. I will be safe…and I need to be alone."

She started to remove his greatcoat, and James held up a hand.

"Please, keep it to shelter you from the cold on your return journey."

Miss Ashford smiled, a barely-there curve of her lips, and murmured, "Thank you, Mr. Delaney."

She whirled around and walked away without looking back. James watched her until she disappeared from his sight. It was only then he continued his journey to the inn.

Almost two hours later, perhaps it could be more, James stood by the window overlooking the forecourt of the inn. He'd taken a bath and had a warm meal but found that sleep eluded him. He held in his hands the letter Richard had given him when they had marched to war.

James stared at it for a long time, wondering if Richard had ever read James's equivalent letter. After their very first battle together, the wool had been removed from their eyes, and they had discovered the harsh understanding of war. They had decided to write to each other, with the vow not to open their respective letter unless the other died on the battlefield. Those letters would contain their unfulfilled wishes and hopes the other should see fulfilled.

They had kept those letters, and though Richard hadn't perished directly on the battlefield, James had traveled with the letter today.

What wish did you have, my friend, that you wanted to be fulfilled?

With slightly trembling fingers James opened the letter.

Dear James,

If all is to be believed, I have perished, and you are now reading my last wish. I do hope you are reading this letter many years from now, when we are old men and married with many children, and the only reason we have opened our letters is to reminisce on the past and the foolish hopes we've long held in our hearts.

If I have died young, I have failed my family. I am the oldest and should provide suitably for my family. If I have left them in the lurch, the one thing I ask for is that you take care of my sister, Poppy.

When my father departed several years prior, he left my stepmother a very handsome widow's portion, and for my two youngest sisters, he provided suitable dowries. It was unfortunate that when father married our stepmother, he only had space in his heart for her and the two new daughters she bore him. He only left Poppy a pearl necklace and a painting of our mother.

Undoubtedly, at this point, you are wondering what I mean by taking care of Poppy. You are the second son of a well-connected family and have many prospects. I am asking you to marry her.

A feeling unknown to James jolted through his heart, and he read that line three more times before he read the rest of the letter.

Poppy is a lovely girl with many admirable qualities, and she is filled with good humor. Whenever I am morose, she has the most astonishing ability to bring a smile to my lips. She is a bit of a romantic, but I daresay for a man as opposed to sentiments as yourself, it is a good balance. You might never love her, but I know you will treat her with kind consideration. I do not want to deceive you by implying she is the sweetest creature at all times. When the situation calls for it, her charming tongue can become the sharpest sword.

I am shamelessly importuning on your connections, and for our friendship, in the hopes, it will find happiness for her.

Your friend,
Richard.

"Bloody hell," James muttered, not understanding why his heart pounded so fiercely.

James released another harsh breath. They had written these letters years before James had become the earl and discovered that the person he would marry was no longer his choice to make. Last year James had told Richard in a letter about the vow Henry had made to a wine merchant, an oath James was honor-bound to fulfill for his brother and family.

My good fool, I am honor bound to marry Miss Vinette Winters.

Yet he had also given his word of honor to his friend that whatever he requested in his letter would be fulfilled.

What a damn quandary.

CHAPTER 2

*Present-day… London.
2 years later.*

The morning was rather lovely, and Poppy inhaled the scent of spring into her lungs. She loved the flowers that bloomed this time of the year. Snowdrops and primroses were her favorites, and a surge of longing went through her for the small and lovingly tended garden she left back in Lincolnshire. Spring was quite her preferred season; winter, of course, being the one she disliked the most. Hurrying up the front steps of her younger sister's townhouse on Upper Wimpole Street, there was a definite bounce in Poppy's step.

This past week, she had interviewed for three different posts—all governess positions in respectable households—and Poppy was extremely hopeful she would secure a position soon. She was four and twenty. It was impossible to continue living under her stepmother's largesse, especially when given so reluctantly and often remarked that it was a burden to feed and clothe her. She wanted to be comfortably established and not obliged to importune any family member who might regard her as 'the unfortunate burden.' Words she'd heard her sister Lavinia use to describe Poppy to her husband.

Poppy was quite determined to make a future for herself that did not rely on the changeable goodwill of others or marriage to a gentleman—not when that prospect for her seemed nonexistent, despite secretly wishing for it so fervently. With a bit of ingenuity and a strict economy, she hoped to live a good life.

The butler opened the door before she knocked, and Poppy smiled her thanks.

"Mrs. Ashford has asked for you to join her in the drawing-room, Miss Poppy."

Poppy paused in the act of removing her hat. "Did mother say immediately upon returning home, or do I have time to run to the kitchen for a spot of tea and some cakes?"

The corner of his eyes crinkled in a smile. "I am afraid it is right away, Miss Poppy."

She unbuttoned her jacket, removed her gloves, and handed them over along with her hat. Smoothing down the skirts of her serviceable dark blue dress, Poppy hurried down the hallway into the tastefully furnished drawing-room. Politely she knocked on the slightly ajar door before sweeping inside. Her two younger sisters, Rebecca, and Lavinia who was now Baroness Hayes, sat on a plush dark, green-colored sofa with their mother, Mrs. Hester Ashford, who appeared faint. Alarm darted through Poppy. It seemed something of a serious nature had happened.

"Mother," Poppy said, for she had learned as a young girl her stepmother must never be called mama. "Is all well?"

"Close the door, young lady!" her stepmother said, rising to her feet. Her stepmother had been the leading belle of her season and was still considered a very handsome woman. If her blonde hair now needed regular chamomile rinses to maintain its color, then at least it did not appear brassy, as if she had resorted to dye. Her once delicate features were currently marred by a scowl, and Poppy knew some delicate lines would be revealed when her maid removed her maquillage. However, it was artfully done, and only those who examined her closely might notice the signs of aging.

Her dove-gray silk gown with the fashionable dropped shoulders was elegant, and the hem was decorated by a wide ruffle of hand-made Brussels lace, a matching collar and narrower bands edged the wide sleeves. Poppy thought that her stepmother would look prettier if she smiled more, but she only smiled when she was viewed by men with a fortune to their name. Her stepmother's eyes were an exceptionally pale blue and could calculate the wealth of a prospective suitor with one glance.

Rebecca and Lavinia, who were beautiful replicas of their mother, also stood, and three pairs of accusing eyes glared at Poppy.

"How could you be so callous with our reputations," Lavinia fairly screamed. "Can you imagine my shock when speaking with my dear friend, Lady Prescott, this morning? She mentioned the most delightful person she had interviewed to become a governess to her children. I had to deny that the Miss Poppy Ashford she met was any relation to my family at all!"

Poppy gently closed the door behind her. "Mother—"

"You could have ruined us with your selfish scheme!" her stepmother snapped. "Until Rebecca is wed, you will not do anything so low as to seek positions!"

Her heart beat so fiercely, it took Poppy several moments to gather her composure. Lifting her chin, she replied, "It was never my intention to embarrass my family, only to seek a living for myself."

"You are provided with enough," Lavinia snapped, her cheeks mottled red with her anger. "Mama is under no obligation to have you continue living with her. And even now I have you in my home in London! Without us, would you have ever gotten the opportunity to come to town?"

Poppy loved her younger sisters and doted on them, even seeing how much their mother spoilt them. Her stepmother had little to no affection for Poppy. Growing up, every degree of attention was paid to Rebecca and Lavinia by their mother and father. They were young beauties everyone in the village spoke about and the matches they would make because of it. The predictions had proven true when Lavinia netted herself a baron who had an income of ten thousand pounds a year.

"I do not discount your generosity," Poppy said quietly, "but it is not enough."

Her stepmother spluttered. "You ungrateful—"

"Mother," Poppy interjected. "I do not say it is not enough to imply that *you* must do more. I simply mean that *I* must do more for my life, which is why I have been trying to secure a respectable post. I am not given pin money. My clothes are from three years ago, and most of them I have sewn myself. I am not a participant in the family's activities, merely an observer."

Being an observer sometimes brought amusement to her life, but there were times Poppy had hungered and ached with every emotion in her heart to be a part of their gatherings and frivolities. "I do my best to repay your kindness by doing the things you ask of me, even when they are the tasks for servants."

"Do not blame us if father left you no dowry! He understood with your lack of beauty, your come-out would be a failure," Lavinia sniped.

Poppy leaned on the door and gripped the doorknob so tightly her fingers ached.

Lavinia sat on the sofa and, with grace, poured tea into a cup. There was a fine shaking in her hands. "Nor will you blame us for not spending our monies on your wardrobe. You had the chance to marry the Vicar Rushworth, and you refused! If you insist on *working*, uncaring of how it will affect Rebecca's chance on the marriage mart and my reputation, you will pack and leave my home immediately."

Poppy felt as if someone had stabbed her through her heart. Glancing at Rebecca, who was eighteen and taking part in her first season, Poppy felt a flare of regret. She had not thought that her seeking a post might ruin her sister's chances.

"I'll be a laughingstock if it is known I have a sister who works as a governess!" Lavinia said, turning away as if she could not bear to look at Poppy.

"If you require me to leave your home, I will do so,"

Poppy said softly. She tried to appear calm, but inside, her heart raced, and she felt as if she would shatter. Not once had her sisters said anything to understand why she had to seek a position. She had nowhere else to live. The manor where she had spent most of her life was occupied by a distant cousin and his family. She lived with her stepmother and Rebecca in a charming seven-bedroom cottage in Lincolnshire.

Poppy had fifty pounds, her mother's pearl necklace, a small painting of her mother, music sheets, and the letters she had exchanged in the last two years with Mr. James Delaney. And his greatcoat, which she sometimes scandalously slept with. Those were all the precious things she owned.

"Lavinia," Rebecca said, sitting beside her sister and clasping her hands. "If Poppy leaves, who will I have to be my chaperone?"

Another piercing ache went through Poppy, and she felt it in her bones. The only value she held to her family was in how they could use her. Poppy almost hated herself at this moment for truly loving her sisters.

"Since you are looking for work, I will hire you," her stepmother said with evident disdain. "Though I provide a roof over your head and food, clearly it is not enough."

"Hire me?" Poppy asked, truly astonished.

Her stepmother's lips flattened. "You will accompany your sister as her chaperone for the season. I will ensure you are compensated one hundred pounds for this duty."

Poppy's heart lurched. "One hundred pounds?"

"Yes."

"No," Poppy said and started to turn away.

"You ridiculous, ungrateful girl! That sum is what most governess's make for the year! And that was the post you were silly enough to enquire after with no thought to the family's reputation."

Poppy stared at her stepmother, another ache rising in her throat, but she was firm when she replied, "I will take no less than six hundred pounds."

Several gasps sounded, ranging from affronted to outrage.

"How outrageous you are," Lavinia said, hurrying to stand beside her mother in support. "Rebecca is your sister! You should happily want to be her chaperone."

"Mother is capable; why am I needed?" Poppy asked softly. Though she knew it well. They wanted to be free to enjoy the frivolities of the season. No one wanted to be watching Rebecca as she walked in the garden with a suitor, or danced with him, or sit nearby to ensure all the proper niceties and decorum were maintained until an offer was made and announced.

Her stepmother was still ravishing herself at two and forty and had her eye on a certain widower viscount. Her ambitions did not end with her daughter. Lavinia had gotten airs since she married her baron, and what elegant airs they were. Their father had been a country gentleman with little connection to the nobility. But the two daughters he had with his second wife had been blessed with great beauty. Lavinia had secured herself a baron without even having a season. They had met at a ball in the nearby small town's assembly room, and only two weeks later, he had offered for her.

What a catch it had been and the talk of the village for

weeks. Lavinia had taken to life in the *haute monde* with ease and grace. Her mannerisms had gotten loftier, her mode of dress vibrant and wealthy, as if she had been born with the golden spoon in her mouth. At one and twenty, she did not want to act as a matron or chaperone to her younger sister. No, Lavinia would laugh and dance and dazzle with the best of them. In their eyes, only Poppy had no prospects, so her time was available for them to make demands. Well, not without compensation. She must plan for her future in whatever manner she deemed fit.

"The governess post offered by the Marquess of Lindstrom pays fifty pounds per month. A very generous compensation to assist in educating his three lovely children. If I am to refuse that post, the compensation must, of course, match." Poppy hoped they would not realize she had not been offered the position. Nor did she have the confidence she would be the candidate selected.

"Ungrateful girl!" her stepmother cried, her lips pinching. "Very well, you will act as a chaperone and a paid companion for the season."

Shock jerked through Poppy. She had not truly expected this outcome. Without her stepmother's largesse, Poppy would not have a roof over her head. They could have twisted that truth to earn her compliance. She stared at them, realizing they truly did not want her seeking any sort of position until Rebecca was safely wed. It was only then she would be dispensable.

"You have decided on the gentleman Rebecca is to marry?"

"Not that it is any concern of yours," Lavinia said with an air of satisfaction, "but we have."

Rebecca brightened, and her blue eyes glittered. "Poppy, I shall think you a simpleton if you cannot guess who I am determined to marry. Why this season's most eligible bachelor. He is young and so very handsome! Not to mention wealthy."

"I am not current with the bachelors of society," Poppy said drily.

Rebecca twirled, her expression taking on a dreamy cast. "I will only have the Earl of Kingsley!"

"There is a ball tonight," Lavinia said. "I managed to secure us all invitations, and I was told the earl might be in attendance. His sister is a popular society hostess, and he often accompanies her to balls and whatnot. Tonight will be Rebecca's chance to meet him!"

Poppy stared at her sister. If anyone could land a handsome young gentleman with such a notable title, it would be Rebecca. She was extraordinarily beautiful with her cornflower blonde hair and bright blue eyes. Her face was also flawlessly designed with a small, elegant nose, gently rounded cheeks, and sensual lips.

"I will require an advance," Poppy said. "At least two hundred pounds. I cannot…I cannot go about in society as a companion with my current wardrobe."

"I have some gowns from last season you could wear," Lavinia said with a careless wave of her hand. "You've lost enough weight since…"

Poppy's stomach clenched. *Since Richard died*. No longer were their barbs accusing her of being overly plump needed. It had taken months after her brother's death to regain an appetite and a determination to live happily. Her stepmother and sisters had recovered from their grief quickly, and even Lavinia had bemoaned wearing mourning garb.

"If you will excuse me," Poppy politely said, turned around, opened the door, and escaped into the hallway.

She inhaled, then exhaled, long and slow. It was not in her to be spiteful and insist she would continue job-seeking, knowing it might affect her younger sister's chances at a good match. But it was most certainly in her to be compensated for her duty. Pushing aside the annoying guilt, she hurried up the stairs and to the charming bedchamber assigned to her.

Poppy hugged her hands around herself tightly. It was just a few more months under the roof of her sibling and parent. Poppy would ignore all their barbs and cutting comments. She would not even mind being asked to stay in her room when Lavinia and her baron had company over for dinner. No, Poppy would only direct her energies into planning for her future, for no one else would.

Her gaze went to the small treasure chest on her vanity. Going over to it, she opened the lid and lifted a packet of a dozen letters. She untied the ribbon and selected the letter she had received last from Mr. Delaney.

Just thinking his name sent a flutter of warm sensation through her heart and an odd feeling to settle low in her belly. Though she had been broken with grief the one time they had met, she recalled the stunning beauty of his dark indigo eyes, the comfort found in the breadth of his powerful shoulders, the way his presence had sucked away the pain and replaced the emptiness with wonderful heat.

Poppy thought of Mr. Delaney often over the years. When she had felt so hollow and broken, his kindness had filled the hole of darkness she thought would swallow her under. There had been a few times she had taken out his greatcoat and slept with it cuddled in her arms. All the emptiness would then flee, and for that night, her sleep was peaceful.

The very memory had her cheeks heating and a wry chuckle slipping from her.

With trembling fingers, Poppy unfolded the letter.

Dear Poppy,

Thank you for letting me know you will be traveling to London soon and that you greatly enjoyed the gift I sent for your birthday.

She smiled, recalling the music sheets and the candied pineapples he had sent for her. Somehow, he had appointed himself a guardian of sorts. He sent rare and wonderful gifts that she hoarded and did not reveal to anyone. Poppy, however, treasured the letters they exchanged more than the gifts.

I still do not think my suggestion outrageous. I would like to purchase you a grand pianoforte. It is not an expensive or inappropriate gift amongst friends at all. When you speak of playing, I feel the passion in your words. I daresay I would like to hear you play one day. Should you arrive in town soon after this letter, please send me a note at my townhouse in Grosvenor Square. I will enclose the full address for you. Perhaps finally we shall meet again.

Your friend,
James Delaney.

Poppy had been in London three weeks now, and she had not sent him any more letters or even a note to Grosvenor Square. There was a nervousness inside her at the thought of meeting him face to face once more. She did not understand it, for nothing untoward had happened at their first meeting.

The memory of being snuggled in his lap, her face buried in the crook of his neck rose sharply in her thoughts, and a breathless sensation swept through her body. She had too much common sense to think a man so well connected and popular as Mr. Delaney might form a tendre for her. It was only a kindness that he had kept up their correspondence these past two years. With a groan, Poppy refolded the letter and put it back in her treasure chest. Surely it could not be over *that* she felt such anxiety searing through her at the thought of seeing Mr. Delaney again.

CHAPTER 3

That evening they were all bundled inside Lavinia's town carriage, rattling away to her dearest friend's midnight ball. Amusingly, Lavinia's friend also lived on Upper Wimpole Street, perhaps a few minutes' walk, but it would be most unfashionable to appear at any ball on foot.

"You look lovely," her stepmother said stiffly, a flicker of surprise on her face.

With a jolt of surprise, Poppy realized the compliment was directed at her. "Thank you," she replied, also noting the assessment of her sisters.

"I never imagined you had such a gown in your armoire," Lavinia said with a tight smile. "However did you afford it?"

Poppy stared at her sister, wondering if she imagined the hint of envy she heard in her tone. Her stepmother and two sisters were dressed in the heights of fashion with rubies and diamonds winking at their ears and throat. Rebecca's silken gown was patterned in tiny clusters of magnolia flowers. It revealed her creamy shoulders and had delicate short sleeves and a corsage of cream silk flowers at the center of the lowish neckline. The hem was inset by a slightly darker cream lace with clusters of peach silk flowers regularly interspersed. It was a beautiful dress and this year's crack of fashion. Lavinia, as a young matron could risk darker colors, had chosen cobalt blue watered silk with a deep frill of Chantilly lace around the neckline and elbow-length sleeves of the same lace above her white satin gloves.

Poppy had darned the white pair of kid gloves she wore, no earbobs adorned her ears, and only a single strand of pearls encircled her throat. Surely that envious tone from her sister was misplaced.

"It was a gift from Richard on my one and twentieth birthday," Poppy said politely, smoothing down the front of her simple but elegant icy blue ballgown with its ruffled sleeves, cinched waist, and scalloped neckline. "Tonight is my first chance to wear it."

"Well," Lavinia said brightly, "See that you adjust the other dresses I sent to you for other outings. They are far more fashionable even if they are last season's wear."

Rebecca heaved a long sigh. "It is the earl we should be speaking about! I am a bit nervous not knowing anything about him."

"I've heard that he treats everyone with bored indifference but owns the right amount of charm to not make him a person non grata," Lavinia said, smiling at Rebecca. "He was a bit of a devil before he inherited the title and had even made Captain in Her Majesty's army!"

Rebecca brightened. "Did you find out why he does not like to attend balls?"

"Some speculate it is to avoid the parson's trap, but he is careful to accept the more notable invitations to keep his connections with notable lords and ladies current. Lady Sarah told me the last three balls he attended, he only danced with his sister. Many hearts were left disappointed. I cannot imagine why he would be so disagreeable at all," Lavinia groused with a sigh.

Poppy lowered the carriage curtains. "Perhaps he does not want to marry."

"Not marry?" Rebecca cried, aghast. "Poppy, your ignorance of high society shows. Every lord needs an heir. Hence a wife! And I will make him a most splendid countess."

Rebecca's excitement plucked at buried dreams inside Poppy's chest and reminded her of a time when she had lain in her bed and dreamed of meeting a beau at a country ball. Or even at church. "What if he is an ogre?" she said to Rebecca. "Deciding whom to marry should require careful consideration. Is he kind? Will he be thoughtful and loving?"

Her sister slanted her an annoyed glance. "It only matters that I'll be a countess! Can you imagine? All of the other debutantes will be so jealous of me!"

Irritation flashed in her stepmother's eyes. "Do not fill your sister's head with ridiculous notions. In time, affection will grow between her and the earl."

The carriage rumbled to a halt, and they quickly descended with the aid of the footman. Several ladies and gentlemen formed a queue inside the front door of the lovely townhome. Unbridled excitement rushed through Poppy. Her very first ball. And such an elegant one too. It mattered not that her role tonight was that of a chaperone; once again, an observer, she was pleased to be a part of the music and gaiety.

They were quickly shepherded inside and into the large ballroom. The number of people packed inside the room was astonishing. She followed at a careful pace behind her sisters as Lavinia and the hostess, Viscountess Balfour, introduced Rebecca to several guests. As expected, a stir went through the throng when they noted her ravishing beauty.

Poppy turned in a slow discreet circle, letting the din of music, laughter, and chatter wash over her senses. Ladies twirled in some of the most beautiful gowns she had ever seen. How elegant they all appeared in their fineries, and with diamonds, rubies, and sapphires winking at their throats. Her senses did not feel overwhelmed but intoxicated with excitement. Ladies and gentlemen milled in every direction, seeming to fill all the public rooms of Lady Balfour's home.

"Oh Poppy, we know it is your first London ball, but please do not appear so gauche!" Lavinia said with a mocking laugh.

"It is rather lovely," replied Poppy with a mild smile as she surveyed the fluted column ballroom ahead of her. Each of the classical columns was wreathed in flower garlands bound by primrose ribbons. Matching drapes were hung around the walls, with floral depictions of woodland scenes. The drapery and primrose theme looked especially good against Lady Balfour's straw-colored dress trimmed with bunches of brighter jonquil ribbons. It did not look so good against the purples and red of the matrons of society, but the paler colors of the gowns of younger ladies were shown off to advantage.

The ballroom was crowded with the floor filled with elegant couples, dancing with such grace that Poppy wished she could join in. She regretted that her position as chaperone and lack of dance training meant that was impossible.

Poppy stood by the sidelines, near a refreshment table and several chaises which seated a few ladies. They appeared much older than the dancing crowd though no less elegantly dressed or beautiful. It did not take long for a few gentlemen to make their way over and seek an introduction to Rebecca, who appeared so natural and lovely as she flicked her fan and responded to their request for dances. She displayed no nerves and radiated with lovely confidence.

"You are doing wonderfully," Poppy said, stepping closer to her sister.

"I am so excited," she said with a light and airy laugh, flicking her fan with studied elegance. "I do believe I might make the match of the season."

Poppy smiled. "I daresay it might be possible. I never knew a town ball would be such a wonderful crush. How many dances have you accepted?"

Bright blue eyes landed on Poppy. "Four so far. I am saving the waltz for Lord Kingsley."

Poppy glanced over at the milling crowd. "Is he in attendance?"

"I do not know! I am waiting for Lavinia's signal."

"And what signal might that be?"

"She will open her fan, and the direction she waves it in will be the earl."

Poppy laughed. "The place is overcrowded. Is it not possible for the viscountess to make an introduction?"

"Things are done differently here than in the country! It is perfectly permissible for the earl to seek an introduction, but it might be frowned—" with a dramatic gasp, her sister stopped speaking.

"Lavinia has unfurled her fan!"

Poppy glanced in the direction the fan presumably pointed and rolled her eyes. There were several ladies and gentlemen, and none seemed—her thoughts crashed and shattered into a thousand pieces. Was that Mr. James Delaney?

Poppy was barely aware of her stepmother and Lavinia appearing by their sides.

"I believe he is coming our way," Lavinia said breathlessly. "Lift your chin Rebecca and square your shoulders. Smile, but do not show all your teeth!"

Poppy's heart raced as a most handsome gentleman drifted closer. It was indeed Mr. Delaney. She took an involuntary step forward and faltered. It might be inappropriate for her to approach him, and it might create a stir and a scandal. And what would she say?

"I think the earl is indeed coming over to us," her stepmother said. "I knew you would attract his attention, Rebecca, where all others have failed so far. Now, remember dear to command an air of mystery when you speak and dance with him."

"Yes, mama!"

Poppy frowned, scanning quickly for the earl. The only

gentleman currently walking in their direction was Mr. Delaney—who appeared so perfectly handsome in a black evening jacket and trousers, a white undershirt with a dark blue waistcoat to match his eyes, and an exceptionally tied cravat. His hair seemed in want of trim, for it curled above his forehead and at his nape in black waves. He looked slimmer than when she had last seen him but somehow harder, as if life experiences had aged him. What had not changed was his raw handsomeness, one that was almost beautiful. He possessed in every languid step the confidence and elegance of a gentleman of stature, of a man fully aware of his privileged position in society and how to wield that influence.

Mr. Delaney stopped before them, and an electric current of unbridled anticipation passed between her sisters and stepmother. An incredible and dreadful awareness seized Poppy, and her tongue seemed to tie itself into knots.

"Lord Kingsley," Viscountess Balfour said, "May I present Lady Hayes, her mother Mrs. Ashford, and her sisters Miss Poppy Ashford and Miss Rebecca Ashford."

It was only then Poppy noted the viscountess had somehow materialized beside Mr. Delaney...no Lord Kingsley. Poppy suspected whatever was happening now might have been planned by Lavinia and the viscountess.

He bowed most charmingly and flashed a smile. "It is a pleasure, Lady Hayes, Mrs. Ashbrook, Miss Ashbrook and Miss Rebecca."

"Lord Kingsley," Lavinia said, dipping into a most elegant curtsy. "A pleasure to meet you."

Her stepmother and Rebecca responded in kind, but

Poppy only stared at him, so many questions tumbling through her thoughts. Had he been an earl when they first met?

His gaze landed on her, and Poppy dipped into a curtsy which felt clumsy. "Lord Kingsley," she said upon rising.

"Miss Ashbrook," he replied. "Would you do me the honor of dancing the next set with me? That is if it is not taken?"

There was a gasp, then silence. It was then Poppy noted he stared at her and not Rebecca. A quick glance showed her family and the viscountess stared at her in varying degrees of shock. "I...a dance?"

"Yes, I believe a polka is up next?" He held out his hand. "I have not partnered with anyone as yet. Would you do me the honor, Miss Ashford?"

But I do not know how to dance, she wordlessly cried, staring at his outstretched gloved hand. "No," she said so softly he might not have heard.

However, his brow arched in surprise.

Another sound reached Poppy, a sigh of relief from her stepmother. The crush of the ball that had felt exciting earlier now felt stifling. The walls pressed in on Poppy, and the sounds and scents were unexpectedly overwhelming.

"Our Poppy is not much of a dancer," her stepmother said casually. "She never took to it, I am afraid."

"I believe Rebecca is free for the next set," Lavinia smoothly interposed. "And she is a most incredible dance partner."

Poppy glanced up to find James's eyes—curiously penetrating, on her. Mortified, she dipped into another quick curtsy. "If you will excuse me, Lord Kingsley. I must urgently visit the retiring room for a few minutes."

Without awaiting a reply, Poppy made her escape through the tightly packed ballroom, for once thankful for her short stature. They would not be able to see where she was headed.

James asked me to dance, and I refused. Poppy's face burned, and she did not make for the retiring room but to the open terrace door leading to the back gardens. Keeping away from the laughter and the lantern lights, she walked to an alcove and took several gulping breaths.

Mr. James Delaney was the Earl of Kingsley. *How was it possible?*

Her heart lurched when someone gently touched her elbow from behind. The touch was so unexpected it surprised a gasp from Poppy. She whirled around, her gaze colliding with the fierce brilliance of indigo eyes. "Mr. Delaney…I…Lord Kingsley," Poppy stammered. "Why…" Once again, her tongue tied in knots. She rarely engaged in conversation with the opposite sex, and when she did, it was to answer passionately asked questions about her younger sisters.

He waved his hand dismissively. "Let us dispense with formalities, shall we? Please, call me James."

Poppy tried in vain to interpret the look in his eyes. There was something tender in his stare but also calculating. Poppy did not have enough experience to understand the emotions in his gaze. "I do not dare be so intimate," she breathed.

He came closer until she could feel the pleasant heat

radiating from his body though he did not touch her. "Why…why did you not tell me you are an earl?"

A quick frown chased his handsome features. "Would it have mattered? I am still the same man…your friend."

A shaky laugh escaped Poppy as her heart squeezed painfully. "We met once and exchanged a few letters. Does that make us friends?"

He pressed a hand over his heart as if wounded, and his indigo eyes glinted with humor. "Do not forget I gave you my coat and walked a few miles in the biting cold to my inn without its comforting warmth."

Oh! Poppy hated that every part of her body felt sensitized and that her heart raced. "Why did you ask to dance with me?"

"The truth?"

Her heart gave a little flutter. "Is there a reason to fib?"

"No."

"Then your honesty is appreciated."

A rueful smile touched his mouth. "I saw you, and immediately my senses crowded with memories of our first meeting. They were so vivid I could hear your sob, feel the weight of you in my arms, feel the softness of your lips against my jaw. And your eyes, you have the loveliest silver eyes. I wanted to see them again. Those were the thoughts which drove me to cross the expanse of the ballroom and ask you to partner me in a dance."

Poppy was so stunned by that reply she had nothing to say. Had she been susceptible to flattery and vanity of self, Poppy might think the earl liked her. The expression in his eyes intrigued her. Poppy never had a gentleman look at her in this manner. As if he found her entirely desirable. Her breath hitched as the awareness flowed through her. James wanted her. Surely she mistook the matter.

"I…Mr. Delan…I am sorry, Lord Kingsley…you are staring." In the most delicate manner possible, Poppy tried to ask what he wanted of her but only sounded like a bumbling fool. Irritated, she huffed out a sharp breath. "Why did you follow me out here? I am not overly familiar with the rules and etiquette of high society, but is this not inviting a scandal?"

"I was *very* discreet. No one saw. I wanted to know why you ran from me."

"Should I dance with you, I would make a cake of myself," Poppy said in an embarrassed rush. "And most certainly embarrass you."

"Why is that?"

"I do not know how to dance," she admitted. "I've only had one lesson from my brother on the waltz, and it was more for fun than any serious instructions."

"You are a gentleman's daughter," James said, his brow lifting in surprise. "Your sisters seemed very accomplished."

"I was not afforded the same opportunities," Poppy said mildly. "Nor am I here tonight to dance and have fun. I am Rebecca's chaperone. It is her you should ask to dance."

"I have no wish to dance with your sister."

Poppy stared at the earl, searching his expression. She was surprised he had not fallen instantly under Rebecca's spell. "I…" Poppy stopped talking, for she truly had no notion of what to say.

"Richard often mentioned that growing up, your greatest wish was for a London season."

Poppy's heart jolted, and she waved a hand in casual dismissal. "That was more a flight of fancy from a seventeen-year-old girl who chatted her brother's ears off about balls and musicales. I am now four and twenty, by all accounts, a spinster and firmly ineligible to be a candidate on the marriage mart. Ladies of my age do not have seasons!"

"Then you are in town only to chaperone your sister?"

"I am also hoping to find a suitable position as a governess in a respectable household."

"You are not in jest?"

"Of course not! I cannot live on my stepmother's goodwill forever," Poppy said reasonably.

"Working as a governess can be a thankless position, one also fraught with its own perils, especially if your employer has roving hands."

Shock jolted through Poppy. "Roving hands?"

"It has been known to happen."

Poppy lifted her chin. "I will ensure it does not happen to me."

Concern flickered in his eyes, and he scrubbed a hand over his face. "Richard," he said with quiet contemplation, "he wanted to see you cared for and protected."

Poppy frowned, recalling that she had mentioned to James about Mr. Rushworth. "Yes, by marrying the vicar. I do not regret my decision if that is what you are asking." Not even when she lay in the dark of her chamber, peculiar loneliness and sadness eating at her heart. It felt decidedly unpleasant to be envious of what others possessed—a charming and adoring husband, children, a happy home.

"Do you not want a husband and children?"

Poppy stared at James, wondering at the intimate turn in their conversation. "Why do you ask me this?"

"I want to know if you will truly be happy as a governess."

"If I had another option, I admit…I admit I…I do not like to dream senselessly nor do I like dashed hopes," she answered impulsively, stepping away from him. Being this close to James made her feel too warm. It was discomfiting because of how much she liked the sensations.

"Miss Ashford…Poppy."

She faltered. "Yes."

"I would like to help you."

"Help me do what?"

"Attain your dreams."

Poppy laughed, utterly startled by the man. "And what dreams are those," she whispered. "I hardly know them, for I cannot afford to allow myself to dream aimlessly. What would you know of them?"

His indigo eyes darkened with unfathomable emotions. "Richard spoke of you to me quite often. Surely you would prefer to be the mistress of your own home instead of working for someone."

"There is honor in working," she said tightly. "Do not look down upon me because of it."

He stepped closer. "I would not dare look down upon you…ever. But I want you to imagine this season…finding a gentleman you admire, one you can see a life of happiness with. Allow me to help."

Her heart pounded so fiercely she wondered if he could hear her heartbeat. "And how would you do that?"

"I would provide you with a dowry of ten thousand pounds."

"Have you gone mad?" she demanded faintly, never daring to imagine anyone could be this generous.

"Richard was my best friend, and you are his beloved sister. I daresay that makes you my sister as well."

I am not your sister, she silently cried, painfully aware of the breadth of his shoulders, how wonderful his clothes fit, the beauty of his eyes, and his carnal handsomeness. "How would I ever repay you?"

"Nonsense. This is not a loan. It is a gift."

She shook her head. "I...having a dowry will not make me eligible to gentlemen of the *haute monde*. I..."

"That is why we will work together to make you eligible."

She choked on an incredulous laugh. "*We?*"

"Why do you sound so astonished?"

"What can you do to make men notice me? I am passably pretty with little to no connection—"

James made a slight gesture with his right hand. "You are beyond lovely," he said with such intensity, he stole the air from her lungs. "One look in your eyes and a man will fall into a space he does not even understand but is fully aware of due to the racing of his heart, and the sensation of tumbling into something greater than himself. Your smile is one of the most radiant I have ever seen, and your hair is like a raven's feather. Lush, vibrant, and beautiful. I dare not comment on the shape of your body in fear of appearing a scoundrel in your eyes."

Poppy took a quick sharp breath. "Do you say this to flatter my vanity or because you have experience of it?" she asked softly, wondering at her boldness in doing so.

He chuckled, yet his eyes were somber. "I dare not speak casually with you; however, I am not ashamed to admit your prettiness makes my heart tremble. Imagine the impact on a gentleman who is seeking a wife."

Poppy did not miss the implication that he was not in search of a countess. Rebecca's disappointment would be most profound.

"And if I do not succeed this season? It would be laughable to suggest at my advanced age to make a try for another season."

"I would gift you the same ten thousand pounds."

Poppy pressed a hand over her chest. "How would I ever be able to repay you?"

"By living happily."

Piercingly warm and undefinable emotions swept through Poppy. "Perhaps I should just take the bank draft now."

"If it pleases you."

They stared at each other until the yawning emptiness which often haunted Poppy late in the nights expanded through her body. Without a companion, children, laughter, and happiness, living life alone cannot be an agreeable life to anyone. "Do you never plan to marry?" she whispered.

Surprise flickered in his eyes. "Eventually, I will marry. Just not for the foreseeable future."

And once again, that odd twisting pain went through her. Despite her curiosity about him, she did not have the right to question him. Perhaps should they grow closer, she might ask him about it. "I know nothing about capturing the attention of a gentleman. I do not dance. I do not paint. I have no notions about flirtations."

"I'll teach you."

Poppy couldn't help smiling at him. "To dance and to flirt?"

His mouth quirked in a sensual smile. "Of course, I am a credible teacher. And we will begin our campaign tonight. We will re-enter the ball, separately, and we will dance."

"No," she gasped. "I might fall on my face."

"We'll dance the waltz, and I will lead you."

"James…"

To her utter shock, he stepped closer, placed his hand on her waist and tugged her into his embrace. Poppy barely heard him as he instructed her on where to hold him in return, and then he swept her off her feet. The sounds in the ballroom were muffled but floated on the evening air like night jasmine scent.

A dance. An instructional one and not as if a real beau courted her. Yet it was a magical moment as she breathed in the sweet aroma of spicy sandalwood overlaying the earl's natural masculine musk. Her head swam a little at the proximity to James's more muscular form.

Poppy could hear her own heartbeat and the sounds of the night. The glow of streetlights in the distance lit up the silhouettes of trees and the outlines of darkened buildings. The moon and stars sparkled in the velvet sky, and Poppy felt as if she were in some gothic romance where the wicked villain would carry her away to distant climes. They spun and swirled to a music of their own. When they finally came to a halt, she was breathing hard, and her throat felt tight. Poppy remained silent, not wanting to spoil the feeling and fearing she would make a fool of herself if she dared to utter a single word.

Then she laughed, releasing the tight tension inside her body. The earl chuckled too, as if he understood the delight coursing through her veins at having done something so simple yet so naughty and fun. For a wild moment, she hadn't been an observer but a participant. Dancing was simply perfectly splendid.

"Your laugh, it is lovely."

And unexpectedly that made Poppy laugh a little bit more before she said warmly, "I believe I can get used to flattery."

"Ah, that was not a stroke to your vanity. It is a simple truth."

Poppy made no reply but dipped her head in an elegant acknowledgment of the compliment. "And how was that dancing?" he asked huskily. "You moved beautifully."

She shook her head wordlessly, still feeling the sensation of his hand on her body.

"I am the Earl of Kingsley. Should I dance with you tonight, you will be the name on everyone's lips tomorrow. Society is fickle, but we can rely on that fickleness for your success. My noticing you will also make other gentlemen interested in you. For the remainder of the season, you will have the influence and connections of my family behind you."

A fierce swell of emotions tore through Poppy, and with

great impetuosity, she stepped forward, tipped onto her toes, and pressed a kiss along his jaw. He faltered into profound stillness, and with a soft sigh, she stepped back, but not before she inhaled his masculine scent of sandalwood and oak moss deep into her lungs, as if she would make it a part of her. "Thank you, James. Somehow I shall repay your kindness."

"I will be deserving of your slap, withhold it."

Poppy frowned. "James, what do you mean by—"

His head swooped down, and he took her mouth with his. Poppy almost fainted from the shock of feeling warm sensual lips pressed to her. His tongue stroked against her lower lip. *Oh, God!* A terribly weak-kneed feeling assailed Poppy. He did it again, and with a small whimper, she parted her lips. He kissed her deeper, startling her by cupping her cheeks in his hands and sliding his tongue against her. Pleasure rushed through Poppy's veins in a fiery burn, and with a ragged cry against his mouth, she sagged into his embrace, gripping the lapels of his evening jacket in a fierce clasp, awkwardly returning his ravishing kiss.

CHAPTER 4

James was lost in Miss Poppy Ashford's taste and the wanton moans of startled pleasure she made, as if with each kiss he pressed against her sensual mouth, she discovered something wonderful and exciting. *Stop. Bloody hell, stop!* He cursed himself silently.

He could not stop. Unexpected yearning made him dizzy and greedy. He was painfully, shockingly aroused and should her eyes lower, the proof of it would be evident, and surely her sensibilities would be mortified. James tasted the innocence in her mouth—sweet, carnal innocence that he had wanted to take and corrupt with raw passion. He'd never kissed a lady with such a desperate, burning hunger before, and it was that knowledge that allowed him the strength to lower his hands and pull away from her.

James raked a hand through his hair. "Miss Ashford…" *What the hell could he say?*

"Yes?" she replied huskily, staring at him with bold curiosity. Her beautiful silver eyes were bright with desire, her lips wet and a bit swollen, her cheeks flushed a most becoming pink. The soft glow of the moonlight and a lone lantern in the distance highlighted the full curves of her young body. Quickly, he did his best not to linger on how delectable and mouth-wateringly sensual she appeared in the icy blue gown which clung to her curves like the possessive caress of a lover.

Meeting her eyes once more, James felt something pierce his heart. Poppy didn't stare at him like she wanted to slap him for his unchecked audacity or administer a well-deserved set down. No…she looked like she wanted to kiss him again. Surprisingly, she laughed, a sweet soft sound, almost one of delight.

He had to offer an explanation. But how could he tell her that for almost two years, his dream of kissing her had haunted him, the feel of her lips just now on his jaw broke his restraint? It would sound just like a damn excuse to act the scoundrel when he knew he could not marry her. "Miss Ashford…Poppy…I—"

Bloody hell.

She kissed him, swallowing his muffled sound of surprise, swallowing his groan that echoed his terrible desire. This time she cupped his jaw in her soft, delicate hands, and though the gloves separated her skin from his, he swore he felt the heat of her palms. Before he could sink deeper into her kiss, with a sweet moan, she pulled away.

"Well," she said a bit breathlessly. "That was most diverting."

A new and unexpected warmth surged through James. "Was it?"

"Yes, as first kisses went, it was wonderful and instructional."

Shock jolted through him. *Her first kiss?* A sudden rush of fierce satisfaction filled him. Should he confess that she was his first kiss in almost four years?

"Are we to indulge in lessons like these in my endeavor to secure a match?" she asked with admirable steadiness.

Amusement at her unexpected boldness rushed through him, but it was not enough to dampen the lust the little imp had caused. James tugged at his cravat, which suddenly felt too tight and cumbersome. "Kissing lessons are not necessary."

"I have heard my sister say that a beau must be allowed to steal kisses. How else can a lady know if she finds a gentleman desirable? Even a friend in the country, Miss Charlotte, has kissed a suitor or two."

He narrowed his gaze at her.

Poppy's eyes widened. "You seem as if you want to throttle me. Is it the idea of me kissing someone else?"

Another jolt of shock hit James, and he took a step back from her. *Bloody hell*. "Are you always this…blunt?"

She canted her head. "No. However, I am… comfortable with you. It is surprising to me as well."

Something heated tumbled over inside him.

Her smile softened, and amusement shifted in her eyes. "And you are also avoiding the question."

"Of course not," he said casually, tugging at the cravat again. "Kissing when done discreetly is a part of courtship. But not kissing like we just did. *That* is not for courtship."

"As I said, that was my very first kiss," she said, her lovely eyes glittering with the remnants of curiosity and want. "I never knew there were degrees of kissing. How fascinating."

"There are." This was a flat, tight reply which discouraged further conversation along this direction.

"So I must not kiss another how we just kissed. Is that what you are saying?"

"Yes," he said quite emphatically.

"What does a kissing like that signal if not courtship?"

"Must you know?"

Her eyes lit up with provocative humor. Did the chit already know the answer and teased him?

A grin tugged at her mouth. "Yes, my lord, I must know. How else must I determine if I am to be on guard or a willing participant? Is there a manual or book of sorts with these instructions?"

Something primal pulsed inside of him, and it was the devil-may-care attitude of his youth that urged him to step closer to her and said, "Such a kiss…it is for…seduction…and ravishment. It is a kiss that communicates lust and hunger."

James wasn't sure what reaction he expected to that admission, but it was not the quiet way she contemplated him with that lush secret smile about her mouth.

"Ravishment," she murmured. "I have never imagined anyone might have kissed me ravishingly. The novelty of it is quite charming."

She dipped into a graceful curtsy, swept past him, and returned to the crush of the ballroom. It felt as if she dared him to come after her. James shook his head and tipped his face to the overcast sky. "You are only here to help make

Richard's dying wish a reality," he said to the night sky. "*Nothing* else."

James waited in the gardens for several more minutes, doing his damnedest not to think about that kiss. He returned to the ballroom as a galop was ending. One sweep of the crush and he found Poppy by the sidelines with her sisters beside her. The ladies were engaged in animated chatter, the youngest appearing a bit mulish in her expression while Poppy radiated patience. The other sister who had married well, Lady Hayes, waved her fan with too much vigor, her posture one of anger.

The young Miss Rebecca would be a resounding success given the number of gentlemen eager to claim her hand in a dance. She was a beauty, but nothing moved inside James upon admiring her. It was Poppy who kept tugging his gaze. She was shorter than most, if not all of the ladies present at tonight's gathering. Her curves were also lush and richly pronounced. She was lovely, intelligent, and only a buffoon in want of a wife would pass her over.

A governess. Not while he was alive. Miss Poppy Ashford deserved much more.

James would dance with her tonight and start his campaign of society seeing her as a very eligible choice. He would ask his sister, Daphne, for help in mentioning discreetly that Poppy had a dowry and was connected to their family. One or two casual remarks in the right ears would have the desired effect, and Poppy's desirability would most assuredly improve. How absurd it all was that they had to resort to such schemes.

James milled around in the crowd, pausing to speak with a few friends. He arched a brow upon spying Viscount

Worsley, the last man he expected to see at tonight's gathering. Society gatherings were not his usual haunts, not when he ran one of the most notorious gambling and fighting clubs in society. James had recently taken a chance and invested in some iron foundries in Manchester with Viscount Worsley and Viscount Shaw. James hoped they paid off soon. The estate his brother had worked so hard to save was not yet turning a profit. James promising Poppy a dowry would see him burning the midnight oil for the next several months to see her dreams realized. And that was just a minor detail compared to the rest of the responsibilities he carried.

"I am not used to seeing you at these events," Worsley murmured, coming up to him.

"Odd," James drawled, "I was just thinking the same thing about you. I assume your lovely wife dragged you by the ears to attend?"

They grinned at each other, and Worsley glanced in the direction of the two Miss Ashfords.

"There is a bet in my books that you will accept the old ball and chain this season. Any insider tips?"

James chuckled. "There was also a bet last year."

"They are determined to speculate on your life. I cannot see why, but I do not object to the profit it makes me."

James scoffed. "Whoever is betting on me marrying soon will lose."

"Are you certain? Just now, I saw the way you looked at that young lady. I came over to distract you from causing a bloody scandal. Such hunger…" Worsley teased, deviltry dancing in his silver-gray eyes. "That kind of hunger is the type that has its hooks inside you, and with each tug, it will become more painful until it feels like death if you do not succumb."

That prediction did indeed hook viciously inside of James. "Rubbish. What you saw was mere admiration for a friend."

"Hmm," Worsley said, sipping from his glass of what looked like whisky. He slapped James on the shoulders. "I know where to lay my bet. And I am putting down a thousand pounds."

James silently cursed when his friend strolled away, chuckling. Was he so obvious in his attraction to Miss Ashford? The waltz was announced as the next dance, and James moved through the crush toward Poppy. Her youngest sister and her mother seemed to be arguing with her, and even from his position, he could see the wounded look in her eyes.

An unanticipated protectiveness rushed through James. Earlier, when she had hurried away, and Lady Hayes had tried to slyly manipulate him into dancing with her sister, he had excused himself without any commitment. Another gentleman might have played the game and accepted the trap. But James had been too concerned about Poppy for that artifice. Now he assessed their unit as he drew closer, noting how alone Poppy seemed though she stood with her family.

Mrs. Ashford spied him first. Her eyes brightened with that matchmaking fervor he had become acquainted with these last few years from the mothers and daughters who saw only his title and assumed wealth. He made a general greeting and then bowed in Poppy's direction. "Miss Ashford, would you partner with me in the waltz?"

Secret amusement lit in her eyes, and to his delight, she held out her hand and allowed him to escort her to the dance floor. There was a startled ripple through the crowd, and James already knew what they thought. Why had he singled her out when he had not danced with anyone these last few seasons. It would give rise to many conjectures, and those bumbling fools might start wondering 'what was it about Miss Ashford that intrigued the Earl of Kingsley.' That curiosity would drive them closer to her, and they would find a lady of graceful warmth, remarkable prettiness, charming wit, and kindness. Only a damn fool would end up not making her an offer.

"I fear I am going to step on your toes," she muttered.

Yet there was a glitter of thrilling anticipation, a hidden spark of longing in her eyes that she simply could not hide.

Her throat worked on an evident swallow. "I can feel *everyone* looking at us."

"It is the novelty of me dancing," he said dryly.

"Ah, so this is a rare and awe-inspiring treat?"

He thought it rather silly himself how invested society was in his pursuits and activities. His sister had brought more than one scandal sheet to his attention, and the content never ceased to amaze James. "Yes."

"Society must be terribly bored."

James chuckled at that dry assessment. The opening strains of the waltz rose on the air, and he slid their elbows alongside each other, and twirled with her. She claimed Richard had only given her one lesson, but she must have been a gifted student. Poppy glided beautifully with him across the expanse of the ballroom, her eyes never leaving his.

James swore she sucked him under into another world, another place and time. The constant worry of executing his duties and responsibilities to his title, family, and tenants fell away. The honor-bound promise he would have to fulfill for his brother three years from now disappeared. The only thing that mattered at this moment was the utter joy radiating from Poppy's eyes as they spun across the ballroom. James had to ruthlessly pull his gaze from her and concentrate on each glide and twirl. Now he understood the pleasure of dancing with a lady one courted.

Except I am not courting her.

The reminder was necessary, and it truly surprised James that a man of his restraint could be so awfully tempted. The dance ended, and she laughed, the sound low and husky, delighted and pleased.

"You enjoyed that."

"More than I thought possible."

Holding out his arm, she gently placed her gloved hand on his, and he escorted her back to her family who looked displeased. James dipped into a short bow, made his excuses, and departed.

James had kissed Poppy, and it was the most pleasant… nay, the most delightful, sweet, and erotic kiss he'd ever had in his damn life. That she had fitted so perfectly in his arms was another unexpected treat. That her smile warmed him was befuddling, and that her eyes felt like they had bewitched him was troubling. James knew within his gut, tonight his dreams would be haunted by her. One thing became starkly clear to him: Whatever help he granted Poppy must be done from a distance, for he could not touch her again. Or he would devour her like a hungry lion.

That would not do under any circumstance.

CHAPTER 5

The very next morning, after a predictably restless night, James sat in the informal dining room, breaking his fast with his mother and sister, who were his guests for the weekend. His mother spent most of her time in Bath, and whenever she came to London, she preferred to reside with her young, widowed daughter who had her own home in Russell Square. She had said some nonsense about 'bachelors needed their space to be bachelors.'

James had asked his sister a few questions on what it would take to improve a lady's prospects within society, and Daphne's answers were in line with his previous assessment.

"I would like to give my support to a young lady of society and wish for your help in this matter."

"You want me to do what?" Daphne asked, surprise widening her eyes.

"I would like your help with a friend's acceptance within society," he repeated patiently. "We will discuss it further after breakfast if that is agreeable to you."

His sister and mother exchanged a look he could not interpret. James took a sip of his coffee, wondering if he would have to work to avoid their matchmaking efforts as well. He would never understand why ladies had to meddle in these things instead of allowing courtship and attachment to occur naturally. It was as if they thought men simpletons who did not know their own minds and had to be led to the altar with manipulations and coquetry.

"You created quite a stir last night," Daphne said, taking her time slathering raspberry preserve on her toast, keenly watching James.

Their mother paused in the act of drinking her coffee and lowered the cup to the breakfast table. "A stir that might appear in the scandal sheets?" the countess asked. "Why am I only now hearing of this?"

"Oh, mama, I am sure it will be in all the scandal rags this morning, and even in the chronicle dear brother is perusing," she said, her voice rich with mirth and such teasing.

James lowered the pressed newssheet he'd been reading and arched a brow at his sister, who had the temerity to wink. "Daphne greatly exaggerates the matter, mother."

Their mother frowned. "Daphne?"

"Mama, he *danced* with a lady last night," Daphne replied with a pleased grin. "Everyone was all aflutter. Imagine, the most elusive and eligible earl of the past few seasons danced with a little nobody from the country and then did as he always does at balls, ignoring everyone else."

"Do not be uncivil or like those petty creatures of the *haute monde*. Her name is Miss Poppy Ashford. She is not a little nobody," James replied.

His mother and sister stared at him with varying degrees of astonishment.

"So, you do know her," Daphne cried.

"Of course I do," he said drily. "Why else would I have approached her?"

"Surely you realize the storm of speculation you caused last night by singling her out for your attention! You've been the earl now for four years, brother, and you have shown no marked attention to any lady from society. This Miss Ashford is rather…plain, if it is permissible for me to say so, but she is the only lady you have danced with in four years! Surely you can understand the rumors that will be running the mill within society."

James leaned back in his chair. "In your considered opinion, sister, did dancing with me improve her prospect with other eligible gentlemen of the marriage mart?"

She took a bite from her toast and chewed thoughtfully. "Men are rather peculiar creatures, and I believe they will be most inquisitive to know why you singled her out, and those who were not interested before will call upon her to satisfy their curiosity."

"Are you not at all interested in this young lady for yourself?" his mother asked carefully.

His heart lurched. "Of course not."

Daphne squinted at him. "Then why—"

James cleared his throat. "She is Richard's sister," he said. "When he died…one of his last wishes was that I took care of her."

His family knew how much Richard meant to James, and they too missed Richard's joviality and the way he would try and charm everyone around him into laughter.

The countess lowered her fork. "Poppy...I do recall Richard speaking about this sister with great fondness. So he appointed you her guardian?"

"There was nothing so formal. She is of age to make her own decisions, even referred to herself as a spinster. Rubbish, of course. She does not look a day over nineteen and is quite lovely."

"We know what Richard means...meant to you," Daphne said softly, lowering her eyes before meeting his gaze. In her eyes, he saw what Richard had meant to her as well.

Daphne had married at eighteen and lost her husband only six months later to an illness. It had taken Richard several months, but he had charmed Daphne out of her doldrums. She had fancied herself in love with him, even though Richard had tried to treat her like another younger sister. His death had crushed Daphne, and she had mourned for Richard too. She also had shown a remarkable disinterest in remarrying though she was only three and twenty herself.

"Miss Ashford's other two sisters seem to be more fortunate in their connections and friendships. The younger one, I believe her name is Rebecca?" Daphne's brows puckered. "She is quite a beauty and is rumored to have charming manners if a bit arrogant at times. I declare a match for her will soon be announced. It will take more work for society to give Miss Poppy a chance."

"I believe Daphne has the right of it," his mother said, curiosity brightening her eyes. "Who are her connections? Are they suitable enough for our family?"

Bloody hell. The matchmaking fever, which had been

laid to rest a few months ago, seemed to have been rekindled.

"Mother," he began warningly. "Do not think of matching me with Miss Ashford. I will marry in time."

"When?" she snapped, evidently irritated.

Impatience snapped through him. "Three years from now!"

Silence fell around them, and he wanted to curse.

"Why three years from now?" Daphne asked, her blue eyes wide and even more inquisitive than their mother's.

"I must excuse myself. I have a lot of paperwork to deal with on a recent investment." James stood, politely bowed, and made his way from the breakfast room. He made his way to his study, a place he spent at least eight hours daily dealing with affairs of the earldom and new business ventures he speculated on. His mother might be appalled to discover that he had bought a few factories in Leeds and Manchester and had hired competent managers to oversee them. Profits had been turning, and the coffers were slowly refilling. He had also reopened the farming estate that supported many tenants and farm workers in Cornwall only these past three months. The villagers there who had been dependent on them had suffered greatly.

He entered the study and walked over to the long drapes and opened them up. Bright sunlight washed into the room, and he shoved open the large windows overlooking a large garden. His gaze went to the snowdrops, primrose, and lilies blooming in their beauty. With a sigh, James rubbed the back of his neck.

A soft knock sounded on the door before it opened. He did not turn around, and his sister sauntered over to stand beside him. They stood there in companionable silence, and with a sigh, she leaned into him, resting her head on his shoulders.

"The flowers are beautiful," she murmured.

"They are Miss Ashford's favorites."

Daphne lifted her head and shifted so she could view his expression. James felt the baffled touch of her eyes on his face.

"They have also been planted at our home in Derbyshire and the manors in Hertfordshire and Kent."

"Poppy mentioned once in one of her letters that they were her favorite flowers. I thought them pretty and ordered the gardener to have them planted in our homes."

"I see," Daphne said with an airy chuckle. "You like Miss Ashford."

"She is very charming and likable."

"But you will not marry her."

James's heart twisted painfully in his chest. "No...I will not."

"You've changed a lot since our brother died, and you inherited the earldom. I recall a time mama despaired about you. You were excessively quick-tempered, arrogant even, and quite a devil with your pursuits about town. There had even been a time Henry threatened to cut off your allowance."

A rush of intense love filled him at hearing his brother's name. How James wished he had told him that he loved him. But his brother knew. Though they had not voiced their affections for each other often, Henry supported James's many wild ideas over the years. "He did cut me off."

Daphne gasped. "He did not."

"Yes, he did, but then he also helped me in purchasing a commission."

They were silent for a bit, each lost in the memories they shared of their brother.

"You changed James, after Henry died. You became serious. You lock yourself in this study for hours each day. You hardly visit your club; I doubt you have a mistress."

"Daphne!"

"Pish," she said, deviltry dancing in her eyes. "I have heard the gossip. Men of your stature are expected to keep a mistress."

Bloody hell. This was not a conversation he ever envisioned having with his younger sister. As it were, James had not taken a lover in years. More than four years. Nor had he the time to miss pleasures of the flesh. The taste of Poppy's mouth and her sweet, hot moans crowded his senses, and he ruthlessly suppressed those memories from resurfacing now.

"I saw you last night, in the gardens with Miss Ashford. You smiled, and there was this look on your face. It reminded me of the time mama learned you were seen climbing out of Lady Southby's bed-chamber."

James inhaled so sharply he almost felt dizzy. "That was years ago! How did you come to learn of it."

"I was eavesdropping," she said cheekily. Daphne's expression sobered, and she searched his expression carefully. "I have never seen you look at a lady in that manner. You were…you were teaching her to dance, and she was laughing, and your…your expression was at once tender and hungry."

Her cheeks pinkened, but she continued, "You kissed her, James. I turned away at once, but I saw…you care for her. And you would not have seen it, but when she walked away from you to return to the ball, she wore the silliest smile on her face, and her eyes were bright with hope and something else I cannot identify. I cannot understand why you would not make her an offer."

James's heart felt like it would pound outside of his chest. "Henry," he began gruffly, then hesitated.

"Henry what?"

"Father was ill for a long time before he died. The estates were not doing well when Henry inherited. There were lots of debts."

Shock widened her eyes. "He never told us. I…I had two lavish seasons during that time."

"It was his responsibility to fix the problem and to care for you."

Daphne pressed a hand to her chest. "Do you think mama knew?"

"No. I did not know it myself until I became the earl."

"Good heavens," Daphne cried. "Henry was just like you now…working for hours. I normally teased and called him a sourpuss for locking himself away for hours."

"The short of it, he had to sell two of our minor estates and some lands that first year, and it was still not enough. Our mines in Cornwall closed, and hundreds lost their livings. The banks refused to extend any more loans, and our name and reputation were not enough for our creditors. Some creditors were owed for more than two years."

Daphne looked faint. "I...I cannot credit that we did not know."

"He worked hard to keep our family in comfort and ignorance."

"And you are doing the same," she breathed, pressing a hand over her mouth.

"I am the earl. The responsibility is mine and mine alone. Henry...Henry was approached by a businessman who offered a deal. That man, Vernon Winters, would extend a loan to Henry. And in exchange, Henry would marry his daughter."

Surprise flickered across her face. "He did what?"

James understood; upon discovering the agreement, he had felt just as poleaxed.

"Did Henry agree to it?"

"How did you imagine he saved the estate that was on the brink of ruin?"

"I...I never thought of it. Whenever mama questioned him, he reassured us all was well."

"Henry borrowed an unmatched sum from Mr. Winters. Over one hundred thousand pounds with the promise he would make Mr. Winters's daughter a countess one day."

Daphne's hand fluttered to her throat. "That is why he was so against marrying. And now...you are also against marrying! Oh, James!"

With a sigh, James pressed his forehead to the cool pane of the window glass. "Our brother gave his word of honor that he would marry Miss Vinette Winters."

"But Henry died! That arrangement died with him. Surely that is most evident."

James sent her a hard glance of disapproval. "Does that absolve this family of his promise when we still hold the monies Mr. Winters loaned? Our estates were made solvent. Most of our creditors, especially the ones clambering for payments, were settled. How do we say the debt is discharged because the earl who made the promise died? I inherited the benefit of that oath made, so I am honor-bound to fulfill Henry's promise."

"I never imagined this is the reason you have not shown any interest in any ladies of society. You are to marry Miss Winters."

"Yes."

"Why haven't you done so?"

"The same reason Henry did not. She is a young chit. At the moment, she is fourteen years of age."

"Good heavens! That means the agreement was made when she was but a child!"

James raked his fingers through his hair. "Many lords and ladies are promised in marriage at even younger ages; why are you so astonished?"

Daphne's eyes flashed. "How medieval and awful for her. To be sold to your husband without any say in the matter because of the social-climbing upstart that is her father!"

James smiled and chucked her under the chin. "I can see that you are ready to do battle, but that is not the issue. I just wanted you to understand what is happening."

"But James, isn't there any way out of this maddening bargain? Can we not pay back the money."

He stared at her. "The estates are still struggling. We barely have any liquidated funds. I would have to sell the next two smaller estates, this townhouse, all the silverware, paintings, and jewelry pieces, and it still might not be enough to pay back all the monies owed, including Mr. Winters's portion. It would sink us beyond reproach or repair. I would eventually marry, and I do not believe the chit will grow to be long-toothed. Miss Winters will be as good a countess as any other."

Daphne stared at him with large somber eyes. "Yes, but will you love her? And would she love you to know she had no choice but to marry you?"

"Those are problems for three years from now," James said grimly. "Right now…right now I want to see Poppy happy. Will you help me?"

His sister seemed as if she wanted to object, but she held her tongue, smiled wanly and said, "Yes."

And for James, that was all that mattered now.

CHAPTER 6

Meanwhile at Upper Wimpole Street...

Poppy made her way to the breakfast room, only to be informed she was needed for a family meeting in the drawing-room. Her stomach made an insistent noise. Poppy hadn't eaten since last evening. There had been too much nervous excitement at last night's ball to eat anything from the refreshment table. Though her family had departed the ball early, the haunting of James's kiss had kept her awake well into the early hours of the morning.

She was tempted to hurry to her stepmother, loathing how she was often reprimanded if she did not respond right away to a summons. Poppy went into the breakfast room, took up a plate, placed slices of ham, bacon, three thinly sliced and buttered toast, and some kedgeree onto her plate. She did not savor her food as she normally did but ate with her stepmother's temper in her thoughts. Poppy drank two cups of tea and then made her way to the drawing-room. A tight knot formed in her belly. Last night the short carriage ride home had been filled with tension. No one had spoken, and Poppy had wisely kept her own counsel. Her stepmother could be wrathful, and it was best to let her stew in the anger she felt at the earl dancing with the wrong daughter.

Poppy entered the drawing-room, noting the stiffness in her stepmother's posture and the tightness about her mouth. Lavinia and Rebecca sat on the opposite sofa, and surprisingly the young baron was also present.

His boyish and wavy auburn hair was neatly groomed, and he was dressed in a narrow fitted tan trouser and a black Newmarket coat. Complemented with a patterned vest of varying colors from sky blue to royal blue and a neatly tied navy-blue cravat. He was dressed for his day and was usually not about the house at this hour. Yet here he sat in the high wingback chair near the large bay windows looking like he wanted to be anywhere but at this gathering. Still, he stood when she entered and greeted her warmly. His piercing green eyes and the sharp angles of his cheeks softening.

She dipped into a small curtsy. "Lord Hayes, Mother, you asked for me?"

The drawing-room was also overflowing with bouquets and vases of flowers. The overwhelming floral fragrances induced her nose to twitch.

"There are three vases of flowers here for you, Poppy," her stepmother said, her voice rich with displeasure.

"For me?"

"Yes. And a Sir Howell called to see if you would be agreeable to a walk in the park."

Poppy glanced around as if she expected to see this Sir

Howell pop from behind the sofa. "I...I am astonished. I am not familiar with this gentleman."

Surely the earl's plan could not be working so soon.

Rebecca had been facing away from Poppy, but now she whirled around, her eyes brimming with wrathful accusation and rebuke. "How dare you, Poppy?"

"How dare I what?"

"You danced with Lord Kingsley," her sister screeched.

"I am quite aware of it," Poppy said unapologetically. "I was there."

"Do you see nothing objectionable in your conduct?" Her stepmother snapped.

Poppy hated these confrontations when they attacked her for some imagined slight. She swallowed past the tightness that suddenly encircled her throat. Her position was precarious, but she could not allow them to be so willful in casting imagined blame at her feet. "Objectionable? Lord Kingsley asked me to dance. My initial refusal could have caused a scandal, but he was generous enough to ask me again. I accepted. What egregious crime have I committed?"

Rebecca's face took on a mutinous cast. "Lord Kingsley is mine! You know of it and still agreed to dance with him. All the papers are talking about the mysterious lady the earl danced with after refusing to stand up with any other lady since he inherited the earldom. *You*...they are calling plain, boring you mysterious!"

Poppy's chest tightened at the united front of her mother and sister in condemning her for accepting a dance with James. God, if they should know that he had kissed her. The apoplexy from that news would probably send her stepmother to the grave.

"You are spoilt and indulged to the point you are outrageous," Poppy said quietly. "You have no agreement with the earl to be so angry should he ask me or anyone else in society to dance. Your conduct is objectionable and ill-judged, and you need serious correction."

Rebecca's eyes widened, and her cheeks flushed a violet red. "You dare censure me! I—"

"I dare!"

Rebecca flounced over and lifted a hand to deliver a slap to Poppy's cheek. With a jolt of shock and alarm, Poppy gripped her hand before the blow landed. "I am your *older* sister, and despite your overindulged and petulant manners, I love you and hope to see you contented. If you are outrageous enough to slap me, I shall return that slap to you, trice."

She dropped Rebecca's hand and stepped back. There was an ugly look in her stepmother's eyes Poppy had never seen before, and a tight band of unknown emotion wrapped its arms around her. "Mother," Poppy began, "I—"

"You will not dance or speak with Lord Kingsley again," her stepmother said. "You will make your excuses whenever—"

A knock interrupted her, and the butler entered upon being bid entrance by the uncomfortable-looking baron. A swell of shame rushed through Poppy that he should witness the discord between their family and the wild ambition of her sisters and stepmother that seemed to know no propriety.

"Lord Kingsley and Lady Daphne have called."

Lavinia gasped, and Rebecca started to pat her hair and smooth down her dress.

"Please admit the earl and Lady Daphne, Mr. Cadbury, and have Mrs. Andrews prepare the finest tea and cakes right away."

The butler bowed and hurried to do his mistress's bidding.

"Poppy, I believe you should retire to your room for the duration of the earl's visit," her stepmother said with a tight smile.

"I believe the entire family should be present," the baron said. "Miss Poppy, please be seated."

Lavinia whirled toward her husband, staring at him as if he were a rotten creature. "Milton, darling—"

"Miss Poppy will stay to meet the earl," the baron said.

Poppy had never heard him speak to his wife in such a firm manner. He clearly adored her, and Lavinia used that knowledge always to the best of her advantage. Now she flushed, lifted her chin, pasted a smile on her mouth and turned to face Lord Kingsley and Lady Daphne, who had just entered.

Immediately Poppy perceived Lady Daphne to be James's sister. Their resemblance was astonishing, and the lady was remarkable in her beauty with her dark hair and indigo eyes, a perfect replica of her brother's.

His gaze casually swept the room, and when it landed on her, a small smile touched his mouth. Poppy's heart raced too fast. She tried her best to hide the reaction she had to the man. Her lips tingled and the spot on her hips he had touched last night burned. Her entire body felt alive and as if it belonged to someone else.

Her reaction was simply dreadful and intolerable.

"Lord and Lady Hayes," James greeted. "Mrs. Ashford, Miss Ashford, and Miss Rebecca, it is a pleasure."

A beautiful smile bloomed on Rebecca's mouth, and she dropped into a deep and most elegant curtsy. "Lord Kingsley, it is a pleasure."

Greetings and pleasantries aside, James sat in an armchair that was conveniently situated closest to Rebecca. Shrewdness glinted in his dark indigo eyes, and Poppy realized he had detected the tension in the room. The housekeeper arrived with the tea trolley, and during the next few minutes, little conversation passed as tea was served. The entire time Poppy could feel the intensity of his stare as it skipped over her face. She dared not look at him, or she would blush like a debutante and not a lady with mature sensibilities. Poppy was sure of it.

"It is so wonderful for you to call, my lord," Lavinia said, curling her hands around her cup. "I was just mentioning to my dear Rebecca that today seems perfect for a stroll in the park. This spring promises to be less dreary than last season."

He flicked a glance to the window and presumably the bright sun outside. "Indeed it is," James said, ignoring the polite nudge that normally would have prompted a gentleman to offer to take Rebecca out for a stroll. "I thought it time I met the rest of Richard's family. He was one of the better friends I've ever had."

"Richard?" Mrs. Ashford cried, her gaze cutting to Poppy and then back to the earl.

"Yes. It is through Richard I first met Miss Poppy a few years ago. When I saw her at Viscountess Balfour's ball, I was very pleased to reintroduce myself. From the amusing anecdotes Richard shared with us, Daphne has always also been keen to meet Miss Ashford."

A collective relief traveled through her sisters and stepmother.

"Oh, that explains the connection," her stepmother said, smiling brightly. "We were all agog that you would single out Poppy. We were all in a tizzy to understand what it meant."

A cunning and decidedly hardened glint entered James's eyes, and Poppy leaned forward.

"I was about to explain it earlier, Mother. I knew the earl as Mr. Delaney, and we have been in correspondence since Richard's death. It was only last night I discovered Mr. Delaney and the Earl of Kingsley are one and the same."

"What a naughty scheme," Lavinia said, skipping her gaze from Poppy to James.

"My title had no bearings on our communications," he said mildly. "Miss Ashford was quite courteous in receiving the news, and I thank her for her generous understanding."

"I was most pleased when James informed me you were in town, Poppy." Daphne took a sip of her tea, her eyes just as calculating as her brother. "I was dearly hoping you would accompany me on a trip to Chatham in Kent, where our stud farm is for a few days. I dreaded going there alone and believe this a most delightful opportunity to acquaint ourselves."

Her stepmother stiffened. "Oh dear, I fear Poppy is quite engaged for the upcoming week! She has agreed to chaperone our Rebecca to a musicale on Tuesday. There is also an outing at Hampton Court on Thursday, I believe. The Marchioness of Elkins personally invited Rebecca."

"How wonderful," Daphne cried. "I've heard the maze at Hampton Court is wonderful. Perhaps I could ask mama, who has been complaining of lack of excitement this season, to accompany Miss Rebecca. Mama would love the company, and I am sure she would like to get to know you better."

Poppy almost smiled at the sly way Lady Daphne tied their hands. To be seen in the company of the countess would be an immense boost in Rebecca's standing in society, and it would imply the family found her favorable.

"I would be most obliged to Lady Kingsley," Rebecca said, smiling prettily in James's direction.

"Wonderful! I will speak with mama about it. Would you be agreeable to accompanying me to Chatham in Kent, Poppy? Please say yes, I would be odiously bored to travel by myself. I have asked James to be my traveling companion, but he insists he cannot leave town for the foreseeable future."

That announcement had Lavinia and her stepmother exchanging pleased glances. Surely they were cheering that Poppy would be away in Kent while Rebecca would be at the side of the earl they were trying to catch. And suddenly Poppy wanted to be away from her family and their machinations more than she wanted to take her next breath of air.

"Thank you for the invitation," she said with a smile at Daphne. "A quick jaunt to Kent seems fun."

Daphne laughed lightly. "I will only be most sorry to miss Lady Bloomfield's ball. It is usually a massive crush and a delight each year. Mama is looking forward to attending. I believe you will also attend James?"

"I will," he said, taking a sip of his tea.

"Will you be attending, Lady Hayes?" Daphne said, staring pointedly at Lavinia.

Her sister flushed, her hand gripping her cup so tightly Poppy feared it might shatter. "I do not believe we received an invitation this year."

Daphne waved her hands carelessly. "I am certain mama will ensure an invitation from Lady Bloomfield arrives before the ball. Mama keeps mentioning wanting the company of a younger person to amuse her. I am sure she would love your company while Poppy is with me, Rebecca."

"Oh," Mrs. Ashford said, looking pleased as if she had been the one to manipulate the circumstances. "We would be most indebted to the countess."

James and his sister stayed for another thirty minutes in which Rebecca attempted to shamelessly capture his attention. He had shown no signs of disapproval at their efforts and was unfailingly polite if a bit dry in his replies. He adroitly rebuffed all nudges or overtures that suggested he walk with Rebecca in the gardens, showing James to be a consummate player in the game of avoiding matchmaking mamas and ladies with ill-intention. Poppy was almost embarrassed by her stepmother's insistence and at one point had hurriedly turned the conversation toward mundane and safer topics.

She excused herself before their departure, hurried up the stairs to her guest chamber, closed herself inside and flung herself onto the bed, burying her face into the pillow. It was with a distant sort of amazement Poppy realized she was laughing *and* sobbing.

Oh, James, how outrageous you are, but thank you!

CHAPTER 7

The following day, Poppy, along with Lady Daphne, three footmen and a lady's maid, departed London for Chatham. The journey did not take that long, and after only a few hours, they arrived at a most beautiful and charming mansion situated on splendidly manicured and well-tended grounds.

On the journey down, Daphne had informed Poppy that James had thought it prudent she received some lessons in how to dance and how to ride a horse. Poppy had not the benefit of receiving those instructions as her sisters had, and apparently, dancing and knowing how to ride were an important part of courtship. In the nights it was dancing; in the days it was promenading or riding horses or taking a carriage ride in Hyde Park.

Poppy had not objected to his thoughtful plans and felt pleased to be away from her stepmother and sisters for a week or two. Despite their incivility and unpleasantness, she had a deep affection for her family, though she found them odious and trying at times. A part of her wondered how successful Rebecca would be in her plans to capture James's heart back in London.

Poppy silently admitted she would not know how to bear seeing James as her sister's husband. Not when Poppy herself had such a yearning for the blasted man. Puffing out an irritated breath, she glided down the winding staircase of the manor toward the ballroom.

Today her dancing lessons would begin. She would learn to dance the quadrille, the galop, and the outdated minuet because, according to Daphne, one might never know when it will be in fashion again. Poppy would also learn the Viennese waltz and the polka.

Poppy entered the large ballroom to find a slim and fairly tall gentleman awaiting her. He bowed when she entered, and there was a twinkle in his brown eyes. He sported a thin mustache, had an angular jaw, and a most elegant nose. His was a handsome sort but did not seem arrogant. In truth, his warm smile immediately put Poppy at ease.

James and Daphne's Aunt Marielle—as she insisted for Poppy to call her—had been in attendance when they arrived. She had traveled across country from Bath at her nephew's behest and was now a spectator to Poppy's lesson. Daphne had been annoyed and mentioned that ladies of their advanced years did not need a chaperone, and she was already a widow. Aunt Marielle was a very buxom woman with the liveliest and most full-throated laugh Poppy had ever heard. She had liked her immediately. Aunt Marielle also shared the same indigo eyes as Daphne and James and their fair coloring and dark hair.

Daphne was also in the room, positioned in front of the pianoforte on a long, padded seat, and when she saw Poppy, Daphne ran her fingers over the key in a jaunty jig.

Pleasure rushed through Poppy, and her fingertips tingled. That was where she wanted to be, seated before the grand piano playing her music, feeling the notes sinking into her bones and soul, taking her to a place where dreams and peace and happiness were found in music.

"Aunt Marielle," Poppy greeted with a wide smile. "Good morning."

"Hullo, Miss Ashford, I am Mr. Benedict Titus," the young gentleman said, walking over to her. "I will be your dance tutor for the next few days. We will start with the more popular dances first. The polka and the waltz. Perhaps we might even get to the quadrille, but you will know enough to soar."

Poppy smiled, dipped into a curtsy, and went over to the man who had extended his arm to her in an exaggerated flourish.

"The polka is all about beats and steps," he said, twirling his finger in the air. "It is fast, dizzying, and most importantly, fun!"

That seemed to be some sort of cue for Daphne to start playing lively music.

"We will be in close proximity. A bit scandalous, I know," he said with a wink, stepping extraordinarily close to Poppy. The hem of her day dress brushed against his fashionably crisp trousers. "Your right hand will be clasped like this in your partner's left hand, like this."

He took her gloved hand, clasped it, and raised it so

their shoulders were positioned almost at the same height. "Your partner's right hand should then go on your left shoulder blade, and your left hand should rest lightly on his shoulder. The embrace should neither be too delicate nor too heavy, but just right. So that when we move…fast or slow, the clasps are maintained."

Poppy nodded. "I understand."

"Now we hold this position, and we learn the steps. One, two, three—right, left-right, and then left-right-left. When I step forward with my left foot, you step back with your right foot."

Poppy laughed when he dramatically cried, "Music!"

And then they danced. Over and over, they moved, full step then two half steps, right, left, front, back. They were slow at first, then after several minutes, they moved so fast Poppy's blood thrilled.

They stopped and she panted, breathless.

"You are a most quick-witted and remarkable student," he said, holding out his hand again. "Let's continue dancing."

Well over two hours later, their dance lessons ended. Aunt Marielle had long lost interest and had called for the carriage to go into the small town nearby. Daphne had played until she complained of cramping fingers to Mr. Titus's disappointment. Poppy's legs ached, but she felt wonderful. She now knew how to dance the polka and the waltz to greater perfection. Mr. Titus was a guest in the manor, and their lessons would resume tomorrow. Poppy was delighted with the lessons even though there was a part of her that believed it might be in vain.

The ballroom was now empty, and she made her way

over to the pianoforte. With reverent care, she delicately ran her fingers over the keys. Skirting around the long wooden bench, Poppy sat and started to play a song that had been a favorite of Richard's. She then moved onto one of her favorites, a sonata by Franz Schubert, the last piece he had written before his untimely death. It resonated with raw and powerful emotions, and Poppy loved playing it. Closing her eyes, she sank into the majesty and beauty of the music, playing for endless minutes. When it ended, she laughed and contemplated what else to play.

"If I had not witnessed it for myself, I would not have believed a second-handed account," a low voice filled with awe murmured.

Poppy stood and whirled around with a gasp, blinking to see James, Daphne, Mr. Titus and Aunt Marielle standing there, staring at her with varying degrees of amazement.

"Poppy," Daphne breathed, her eyes wide and bright. "You…dear heavens, I have never heard such beautiful playing."

"She is self-taught," James said, his tone rich with warm admiration. "You were simply wonderful."

Poppy's cheeks heated, and she canted her head. "Thank you…whatever are you doing here, James?"

Aunt Marielle raised a brow, and Poppy flushed.

"Forgive me. I meant Lord Kingsley."

"We all knew what you meant, gel," Aunt Marielle harrumphed, but there was a decided twinkle in her eyes. "And now I believe I understand why my nephew is here." She whirled around and withdrew from the ballroom, taking a smiling Daphne and Mr. Titus with her.

Poppy was mortified. "I think your aunt believes there is some sort of tendre between us. You must hasten to correct her."

"My aunt is simply mischievous," he said dryly, but there was a very curious tint of color on his cheekbones.

A warm flutter went off in Poppy's belly. "I thought you were to stay in London?"

"I bought you some apparel and wanted you to have it right away."

"You bought me apparel? I believe you are determined to be scandalous. A most improper gift for any gentleman to give a lady."

A rueful smile curved his mouth, and he bowed. "I am duly chastised; however, as we are…" he seemed to search for the proper words, and Poppy's heart tripped several times.

Did he too wonder at the feelings brewing between them that they evidently did not speak about?

"Yes…we are partners in adventure and friends. I thought it a rather appropriate gift."

A rather peculiar warmth bubbled up inside of Poppy. "Well…what is it?"

"A shawl."

"This shawl could not have waited to be delivered until I return to London?"

"It is a lovely shawl. I have also taken the liberty to impress upon Daphne that she retains her modiste to make you a new wardrobe. At least five new ballgowns, day dresses, hats, laces, and all the assorted fripperies."

Her stunned silence prompted him to say, "I also

wanted to check in with you, of course. A lovely opportunity to kill two birds with the same trip."

She arched a teasing brow, and amusement rushed through Poppy. "Perfectly logical. You needed to check up on me a day after since we last saw each other?"

He grunted a noncommittal reply.

"Is it possible Your Lordship missed me?" Poppy took a few steps closer to him. "Why, that is perfectly understandable given we did not get a chance to converse privately."

His eyes flared then warmed with humor. "You are incorrigible."

"And you are blushing," she said in soft wonderment.

The fluttering in her stomach increased with such intensity Poppy pressed her hands to her waist, squeezing it in hopes of stopping the disordered sensations erupting there. They were entirely too new and unexpected. Deeper than anything she had ever felt before.

James made a choking sound of indignation. "Gentlemen do not blush, and I, for one, have *never* blushed."

Poppy grinned, for the tips of his ears got even redder. The earl glared at her before his expression smoothed into careful indifference.

"I must complete some work in my office. I look forward to seeing you at dinner this evening." There was a slight hesitation, then he said, "I am returning to town tomorrow morning."

A secret thrill went through Poppy's heart, and she silently said, *it has only been a day, but I missed your company as well.*

The intensity of his gaze sharpened, and it was her turn to blush, for Poppy feared he had seen what she felt in her stare. She dipped into a polite curtsy and hurried past him, making her way up the winding staircase to her chamber. Once inside, she leaned against the door.

"I simply have to accept that whenever I see James, my heart will act in a most unruly manner," she muttered to the empty room. *And hunger opens throughout my entire body. A hunger I barely understand but so desperately want to explore.*

James Delaney was so far above her that he might as well be a star in the bespeckled night sky. *Do not dream or hope foolishly,* Poppy reminded herself. Still, there was a smile on her mouth and a hitch in her heart as she went over to the armoire to select a comfortable day dress for a walk in the woods.

CHAPTER 8

Is it possible Your Lordship missed me?

James rolled over in his sleep with an irritated grunt, formed a fist, and slammed it into the pillow. This was perhaps the tenth time he was thumping out his frustration on his bedsheet, cushions, and coverlets. Why in God's name was he so taken with Miss Poppy Ashford that he would lose sleep, that she would appear in his dreams, that he would continually wonder what he could do to surprise her. Just to see that smile bloom on her lips and the joy flash in her dark silver eyes.

"Damn stupid," he growled into the well-padded and scented pillows.

Is it possible Your Lordship missed me?

Hearing that softly amused and astonished question for the eleventh time had him rolling over, casually placing his forearm against his forehead. She was right. He had felt some sort of baffling sensation of missing her. Surely only because he felt as if they had much more to discuss. After leaving Lady Hayes's home on Upper Wimpole Street, he had felt the keenest regret that he had not spoken with Poppy. It had taken the strictest of willpower to have kept going without asking for a private audience. That would have probably created more tension with her family. It was evident to James that Mrs. Ashford did not treat Poppy with the same love and kind considerations as her daughters. Observing the tension between them and the ways they had all glared at Poppy had doubled James's determination to see her settled and contented with her lot.

But that should have nothing to do with the cravings which had erupted through his body that night. Those same cravings torment him even now.

"It was the damn kiss," he muttered, pushing up, and swinging his feet over the bed. "I should never have kissed her, and there will be no bloody lessons in flirtations or seduction."

Sleep would once again elude him. This had been the same damn disease that had troubled him after the first time he met her. For weeks, nay for months, he had thought of that afternoon, of Poppy in his lap snuggled in his arms while he held the umbrella over their heads. The kiss…the bloody chaste and insignificant kiss she had pressed to his cheek had been the most persistent specter of his peculiar torment. He would feel the phantom brush of her lips against his jaw when he slept, read a book, tally the ledgers, ride his horse, read the account books and investment reports.

Is it possible Your Lordship missed me?

James raked his fingers through his hair, and with an irritated grunt, stood and padded to the windows. He had left the drapes drawn, and he stared out into the darkness, wondering what to do about the feelings brewing inside for Miss Ashford. James had been without a lover for over four years. His recent state of constant arousal urged him to procure a lover. But everything inside him recoiled at the notion. That itself was a frustration. The person he wanted to kiss and to seduce into his bed was the very one who had cheekily suggested he blushed and missed her.

What was it about her that enticed him to want to bed her without thought of the consequences? "That is why I must bloody stay away from you," he muttered, thoroughly aggrieved. He must not let the desire linger or give it a chance to develop into a maddening desire that had to be quenched.

Too late.

"What is too late?" he grumbled. "I am the master of my damn self!"

A flash in the dark snagged his attention, and he dipped his head, squinting at the slight figure running toward the eastern section of the lawns.

What the bloody hell?

A bright half-moon splayed in the sky, but it was enough to illuminate the short figure running across the lawns, a stream of wavy black hair floating behind her like a banner. She held in one hand a basket and in the other a lit lantern.

A powerfully unknown sensation rippled over his skin. "What mischief are you doing?"

James was bloody worried. What if this need he wanted to vanquish was already buried deep inside, and he only needed this peek of her running across the lawn toward a gazebo for it to burst forth—peculiar happiness and such yearning he feared it might never be sated. And it was all for Miss Poppy Ashford. A barely pretty and remarkable woman…

Bloody hell. *No, she is beyond remarkable and so damn pretty and provoking*.

He laughed at the awareness he was arguing with himself. Soon he might be a candidate for Bedlam. *God*, he should be avoiding situations like these with her, but he'll be damned if he could. James hurriedly dragged on his stockings, trousers, grabbed his banyan and slipped it on, cinching it tightly at his waist. Moving with stealth, he opened his door, padded down the hallway and the staircase. He exited the manor through the front door, careful to ensure he made no noise. The entire household was asleep, save himself and the reckless imp outside on the lawns.

The feel of the cool night air washed over him, and James thought perhaps he should have donned a shirt or at least put on shoes. Even with his stockings on, the grass was prickly under his feet, but he ignored the slight discomfort and strolled in the direction he saw Poppy headed. His hesitation was drowned by a faint giddy anticipation, though he felt he drifted toward his peril lured by his Poppy siren.

He rounded the corner, and there she sat under a large gazebo, such beautiful flowers surrounding it and trellis on the edges. She hummed a song beneath her breath, and the closer he drew to her, he saw what she unpacked from the basket was food.

Within a few feet, James faltered. She wore the coat he had left behind over her white nightgown, which he could see, for she had not belted the coat. Her thick, curling hair tumbled down her shoulders to her waist in a shimmering curtain of midnight beauty.

He must have made a sound for her head snapped up, and her eyes widened with delight. That immediate and artless joy in seeing him had his throat drying. James stepped closer.

"An art of reeling in a husband is not to wear your heart and emotions on your sleeve."

She arched an elegant brow. "This is a decidedly odd and unexpected topic of conversation."

"It is important not to be obvious with your affection and desires for any gentleman," he said, walking up the few steps of the gazebo. "Just another lesson."

Humor sparkled in her eyes. "I see. I shall keep it in mind should gentlemen truly start to flock to my side."

He sat on the bench farthest from her and lifted his chin to the basket. "A midnight repast?"

"Oh yes, most kind of you to join me." She dipped into the layered picnic basket and removed a small plate with candied pineapple and a round cake with strawberry preserves topping it. A second plate revealed some sort of tart. "Will you join me?"

"I do not recall these foods at dinner."

A quick grin in his direction once again had that warmth traveling through his entire body.

"I made these."

Astonishment lanced him. "You know how to cook?"

"Is that so surprising?"

"A bit. Your father was able to afford a cook and

several servants. It is an odd skill for a young lady to acquire."

She popped a piece of candied pineapple into her mouth and sighed happily. Poppy held out one to him, and he got up and took it from her before returning to his seat. He took a bite, enjoying the tart yet sweet flavor.

"However, did you learn to cook?"

"After papa…after my father passed on, it was most difficult to get the dishes I enjoyed on the menu. All meals were catered to mother, Lavinia, and Rebecca's tastes. Richard ate whatever was on the table," she said with a chuckle.

Poppy looked away briefly, and he noted she played with her hair, twining several strands around two of her fingers. A nervous gesture, perhaps.

"I enjoy fish dishes and the varied way they can be prepared. I like sweets and cakes. Mother berated my… generous figure and ordered our cook not to make them. Or if they are made, I am not allowed to have them. It was ill-mannered of me, but after a year of this, I grew frustrated. Our cook took pity on me after finding me in the kitchens trying to make something I enjoyed. It became a ritual where I would wake up exceedingly early and meet her in the kitchen for lessons. It was wonderful, really, and after several weeks, whenever I felt the craving for a particular food, I would make it and have a picnic on the lawn."

"An evening picnic?"

"The best time to avoid being caught."

"No one here would dare berate you."

"I dare not think so," she said earnestly. "In truth, it

has become a habit, and I find a peace...a joy in it. It also feels a bit free and naughty to steal out into the night and sit by myself. When I am the mistress of my own home, I shall do this without any anxiety of being rebuked as improper."

James liked that her stepmother's indifference had not stifled Poppy's rebellious spirit of joy for living. Many would have crumbled under constant criticism and restrictions. He recalled how often Richard had explained that he doted on her most because all the love from his father had been diverted to his new wife and their two precious daughters.

What a damn ridiculous man, James thought a bit viciously.

"You lost your mother at an earlier age," he said gruffly.

She sent him a considering glance. "I did. I was barely a year old and Richard four years when we lost mama."

"I am sorry you did not get to know her."

Poppy smiled softly. "I did in some ways. I have a portrait of her. Mama was so very lovely. She had the kindest smile and eyes I've ever seen. Father left it to me. He was a bit...distanced, but whenever I asked him about her, he took the time to tell me such wonderful stories."

Thank God the man hadn't been a complete fool.

"To inherit the earldom," she began tentatively. "You lost your...father?"

James cleared his throat. "My father had already died several years ago. It was my brother. He...he collapsed in his study."

"It must have been most difficult to bear."

He grunted softly. "Death is never easy, though it is expected. We have both had our share of it. A damn horrible thing to have in common, wouldn't you say?"

She stared at him with an expression he could not decipher. Poppy stood and made to walk over to him.

"You stay right there," he ordered. Unless there were others about, he would not get within six feet of the damn woman. Not until he found a solution for his malady.

Surprise at his sharp tone blossomed over her face. "Please explain your command. Is everything well, James?"

His throat was uncomfortably tight. It was disorienting. "Yes. We will converse with this space between us."

Despite bare light from the lantern and the pale moonlight, awareness flashed in her silver eyes. They were their own spark in the darkness, rare and beautiful. But she knew what he meant, and a tinge of pink colored her cheeks.

"I love the countryside," she said softly, sinking her hands into the pocket of his greatcoat. "Not only do I sneak from my bed to tinker around in the kitchen and cook. Often, I would go outside on the lawns, run as fast as I can with my hands held wide away from my body and scream."

"Scream?"

She laughed lightly. "Yes. To release all the frustrations I felt in the day. After a few times of being out here, it became another ritual of peace...or joy. There is a sort of defiant freedom of being outside, fully awake while the rest of the world sleeps."

He leaned on the back of his bench and crossed his

feet at the ankles. Her gaze followed his actions, and she smiled at his stocking-clad feet but made no comment.

"It is well after midnight, closer to two in the morning. Are you never afraid?"

"Of what?"

"An unexpected visitor."

"Well, we hardly get those in the countryside." Poppy took her hand out of her pocket and did a very silly action of lifting her hands in the shape of claws and wriggling her fingers. "Or did you mean like a *ghost*?" she asked in an exaggerated whisper.

She was laughing at him, and unexpectedly James found himself smiling. Her sweet laugh sunk deep inside his bones, filling him with a warmth that banished the chill of the night.

"When I first saw you running across the lawns with your hands held open…I admit for a wild moment I thought you were Mary."

"And who might Mary be?"

"The ghost that roams the halls and chambers of our manor and who sometimes traverses into the woodlands. Daphne did not tell you about her?" James asked, breaking his rule by standing and drifting a bit closer to her.

"Daphne most certainly did not," Poppy said, eyeing him skeptically.

"Mary is our Scottish great-great-great-grandmother. Once your room gets very cold, it means Mary has come to visit you. You'll see her in the hallways or by the lake, a lady in a white dress, red hair loose and flowing over her shoulders. She would be singing, and once you hear it, it never leaves you. Mary has the loveliest voice, singing in

Gaelic—haunting and mournful. Once you see her…and feel her sign…" James mock-shuddered.

Poppy's eyes were wide and rapt with interest. "Her sign?"

"Yes, Mary tickles a part of your body."

Poppy's brow puckered in a frown. "Why would she do that?"

"I can only tell you the tale as I hear it."

"Where does she touch?"

He leaned in, lowering his voice. Predictably, Poppy leaned closer. "Mary tickled her victims' left ears."

"Victims!" Poppy gasped, then released a muffled shriek, slapped at her ear, and whirled around.

James quickly dropped his hand and dropped the flower petal on the ground, taking several quick steps back from her. "What is it?"

She turned around slowly and narrowed her eyes at you. "You *beast*!"

"What is this accusation about?" he drawled.

"You tickled my ear just now."

James affected a show of surprise. "Do not be daft. How would I have managed that? Do you hear any singing?"

To his everlasting shock, she launched herself at him and wrapped her hands around his neck. "Confess, or I shall kiss you."

CHAPTER 9

"You...You...bloody hell!" James was spluttering. He never spluttered. He was a man of confidence and self-control.

Confess, or I shall kiss you.

He glared down at the little baggage in his arms, shocked that he could feel the imprint of every luscious curve across his body. This intimately close, the subtle but fragrant scent of her invaded his senses. The feel of her fingers against his nape sent a spark of want through his entire body. His mouth watered. Breathing this close to her felt...impossible. James could not catch his breath. She knew he wanted to keep his distance and was using it to her diabolical advantage.

"Have you no sense of propriety?" he hissed, angrier with himself than her, for every damn sense had come alive in his body. His heart and his cock pounded with lust and such hunger it almost scared him.

"Nay," she hissed back at him, albeit more teasingly. "Spinsters long past the blush of first youth tend to lose those somewhere around four and twenty." Then she tipped onto her toes and pressed her lips against his.

James actually trembled, and it soothed him to feel her lips also trembling against his. His Poppy was uncertain. James parted his lips on a groan, and to his shocked delight, she ran her tongue over the seam of his lips.

"Who taught you that?" he murmured against her mouth. "Tell me right away, so I might put a bullet in his black heart."

She giggled—but it did not sound sweet and simpering but throaty and sensual…the soft puff of her breath teasing his lips. "I would only dare do this with you…my partner in adventure, and my tutor in flirtations and…kisses."

She nipped at his bottom lip and then soothed it with a soft suck. His entire body flushed hot and then went weak.

"I read this is a most flirtatious kiss a lady can enjoy with a gentleman."

He framed her face between his hands, tilted her head slightly, and for several seconds ravished her mouth most thoroughly. James slid his tongue against hers, nipping at her lips, and then repeated the motion over and over. It was when she moaned and sagged against him, clutching at his shoulders, that he lifted his head. Her well-kissed lips glistened. Poppy leaned back, her chest lifting on her ragged breaths. They were both breathing as if they had chased each other around the gazebo.

James lowered his hands slowly. "What book are you reading?"

She dipped into the pocket of his coat and withdrew a small object. *A Guide to Passionate Romps between a Lord and his*

Lady. This book was written by a gentleman of society, and it had been a great scandal. James vaguely recalled the furor, for he had been too busy learning the ins and out of his earldom. If his memory served him right, it was written by an earl, Lord Kentwood, and this book was rumored to be naughty and most salacious.

James stared at the book for several moments before glancing up at her. Her cheeks were bright red, and her chin was lifted in a defiant tilt. "This book belongs to you."

"Yes," she replied innocently, so much at odds with the daring provocation in her eyes. "We spinsters have the liberty to read such work. It is delightfully enlightening."

He choked on air. James did not need to wonder why she would read this. Poppy was a woman of four and twenty, not a chit wet behind the ears. Her sensuality had been sparked, possibly by the bloody kiss which haunted him. And knowing her inquisitive nature, she would seek to assuage her curiosity. Thank God it was the book. A part of him was not ready as yet for her to find a suitor.

Not yet. Not yet. Bloody hell. "Poppy…"

"Yes."

He cleared his throat and handed her back the book. "I do not think it wise for us to have kissing lessons."

Her cheeks burned a bright red, and some of her earlier sensual confidence leaked away. She gripped the book in front of her as if it were a lifeline.

"You say this because I am a terrible—"

"I say this because I want you so desperately. I cannot be an objective teacher. If I keep kissing you…I might ravish you. And it will be a thorough ravishment, and I…I cannot marry."

She blinked and then graced him with a most dazzling smile, rocking him back on his heels. "I know," she said softly. "Not until three years from now. I will be long wedded by then and possibly with a child."

The image that leaped to his mind had him closing his eyes. They were at once beautiful and torturous. Poppy walking across a lawn, a toddler running behind her, both chortling. However, the man to run up and gather his family was not James.

"Yes," he agreed gruffly, then quickly added. "But you will not learn from anyone else. Until you are married, no kisses."

Poppy laughed, and the way she stared at him, it was as if she knew something James did not and was thoroughly delighted by the knowledge.

"I will stop your ravishment," she murmured.

"Poppy—"

"Should you kiss me, and because it is so lovely you decide you *must* ravish me, I will press my fingers over your lips like this, which means I'll go no further," she whispered. Then she did it, placing two of her fingers perfectly over his mouth. "And you'll stop because you are a man of honor."

A chuff sounded from James. "Of course I will. I think I quite made out gentlemen to appear like ravaging beasts who cannot control their baser impulses. But I assure you I overstated the matter. Though you are a delightful temptation, I am in control of my passions. Many gentlemen are."

Her eyes lit up with pleasure. "A delightful temptation; I like the sound of that."

What a teasing minx.

"Now, James, does this mean you'll teach me about all the types of kisses and whatnot?"

James smiled, and acting on the impulse driving him, dipped his head slightly and pressed a kiss to her forehead. Then he replied, "No." James turned around and walked away, shaking his head at the laughter coming from her.

The little minx enjoyed that she had tied him in knots. He imagined that she would be pleased after believing herself an ugly duckling for so long. James's inability to control his passions around her titillated her ego. The woman in her was fascinated. And he couldn't begrudge her, even if he wished he were not so obviously, desperately attracted.

"Good night, Poppy."

"Good night to you too, James," she replied directly behind him.

If he were a lesser man, James would have jerked and betrayed his startlement. With a grunt, he paused, allowing her to come to his side.

"I will be leaving in the morning."

He felt the touch of her eyes on his face as they searched his expression.

"I will miss you," she said softly. "You are a very good friend."

He made no reply, but his heart started a fierce pounding. *I will miss you too*. They walked back to the house in companionable silence, with James thinking he had never had a more wonderful encounter.

Over the following days, Poppy had regular dancing lessons, enjoyed pleasant walks around the grounds with Daphne as the weather stayed fine, and then spent hours at her music practice. Usually, the others drifted in to listen and enthuse over her playing. But today she was summoned to the small parlor. Upon entering she encountered Daphne and a woman of indeterminate years.

"Poppy, dearest, this is Mrs. Pearson, who is my modiste. You need a riding habit before you can start riding lessons, so she will take your measurements. I think as your feet are so small that a pair of my mother's old riding boots will fit you for now, and we can have new ones made when we return to town."

Poppy curtsied and smiled her greeting at Mrs. Pearson before turning toward Daphne. "A new habit," Poppy said, wrinkling her nose. "I very much doubt I will be doing much riding when we return to town."

"I believe you will," Daphne said encouragingly. "My brother is very smart and mostly always correct. Gentlemen will flock to your side upon returning to town."

Poppy grinned. "I shall like to see that. James had promised to return here to accompany me on a few of my riding lessons. Do you believe he will return soon?"

Daphne sent her a considering glance, and Poppy fought the blush rising in her cheeks. *Drat*. Perhaps she tried to sound *too* nonchalant.

"My brother did not inform me when he will return. I do hope it is soon. Things are much livelier when he is here."

Poppy made a soft, noncommittal reply. "I am not at all certain riding habits are necessary. At least new ones."

Daphne pursed her lips. "Our body shapes are so different that my habits would take considerable altering. So, it seemed more sensible to have one made up for you."

"Thank you; that is so very kind of you." Poppy smiled, then turned to face the modiste. Mrs. Pearson was an elegant, well-corseted lady with immaculately coiffured hair and dressed in an elegant black gown trimmed with white lace. The overall impression Poppy first had of her was of stern precision. An impression that was soon proved incorrect as that lady chatted amiably about society scandals, her beloved children, and the latest fashion modes with her.

She did not ask about Poppy's preferences for color or styles but rather stated what colors complement Poppy's complexion, hair, and eyes. And Poppy was happy to leave such decisions to her.

Three days later, Poppy headed up to her chamber to change before going for another walk with Daphne. As Poppy entered, she noticed laid out upon her bed was a cherry red riding habit with golden frogging and tiny buttons. Daphne's maid entered and curtsied, "Please, Miss, I was instructed to get you changed into your habit for your riding lesson."

Poppy eagerly changed into the exquisite riding habit and allowed the maid to arrange her thick raven tresses high upon her head. Finally, the maid fixed an artful piece of millinery magic with sweeping red feathers draped coquettishly atop her luxuriant curls. Poppy was bubbling with excitement as she tripped down the stairs to race to the stables.

"Fernley," she cried, calling out to the head groom of his lordship's stud farm. "I have come for my lesson."

Fernley appeared leading out an exquisite black mare supplied with a sidesaddle of the best Spanish leather.

"Oh, she is so pretty," Poppy exclaimed as she stroked the mare's mane.

"His Lordship chose her specially for you, Miss Ashford. She is a gentle lady, for all her high-bred airs," Fernley said, obviously proud of his charge.

Poppy stiffened. "His Lordship?"

"Yes."

Her heart started to drum a fierce beat, and flutters went off low in her stomach. "His Lordship is here?"

Before Fernley answered, another groom appeared, with a white-faced bay stallion on a leading rein. Poppy moved over to admire the fine stallion. Fernley sneaked her a carrot for the horse.

"He is stunning," she breathed. "And powerful."

"His name is Gallant," Fernley said as the horse whuffled the carrot from her extended palm. "He is His Lordship's horse."

Another spark went off in her heart, and she glanced around.

"Don't spoil him too much, Miss Ashford. He is a greedy brute," James drawled, walking over to scratch between the stallion's ears fondly, negating his stern words as he affectionately caressed his horse.

Poppy hardly knew how to keep her countenance. She slowed the rapid shallows of her breathing before she looked up at him. James was dressed in a deep midnight blue jacket, with tan riding trousers and well-polished Hessians. *How handsome you are.* And for the first time, she was glad for the prettiness of her red habit, which shamelessly flattered her curvaceous figure.

To reveal the pleasure she felt at seeing him was just not done. Yet there was a gleam in his indigo eyes which bespoke a similar delight in seeing her. The smile bloomed on her mouth, and she dipped in a quick curtsy. "My Lord, it is…good to see you."

"It is wonderful to see you as well, Miss Ashford."

How polite he sounded, yet his eyes as they skipped over her were hungry. His awareness of her sent a surge of shock through her entire body. His lashes lowered, and when his gaze lifted to hers, only polite civility stared back at Poppy.

Still, warmth fissured inside and spread throughout her body. Her lessons started, and he was most instructional, his knowledge even greater than Fernley's. Soon Poppy was helped to the mounting block, seated sidesaddle on the horse and was gently trotting. At first, it felt like she was a great many miles from the ground, and she would surely fall on her face and break her neck. However, after several minutes, Poppy relaxed, and the horse seemed to sense the lessening of her tension. They seemed to move as one, and she lifted her face to the rays of the sun and inhaled the crisp morning air into her lungs.

"Give her a little more freedom," James said from where he trotted beside her with graceful ease.

Poppy grinned and urged her horse a little faster. "Oh!" she gasped, gripping the reins as she bounced in the saddle. A surge of worry went through her, but James's quick glance showed only confidence and an at-ease expression. Poppy slowly released her held breath, relaxed her shoulders, and moved with the horse's rhythm.

"Riding is glorious," she said after several minutes, laughing. Poppy never imagined it would have felt so free. This was even better than running across the lawns or dipping in the lake when no one watched.

James's mouth curved into a grin. "You are a natural, just as I suspected it would be."

They trotted about the lanes of the estate until Poppy felt an ache in her rump. Without having to say so, James declared her lesson for the day over. He dismounted from his horse, came around to her, gripped her hips and helped her down. Poppy had the oddest sense of an electric shock going through her body. But staring at his face, all she saw was cool civility. With a swallow, she stepped back from James as soon as her feet touched the ground.

It was painfully uncomfortable being this close to him.

Brushing at the skirts of her habit, she turned away from him, for suddenly he needed not to see that she wore her feelings on her sleeve. Poppy had missed him dreadfully these last few days and had done much to occupy her thoughts, so she did not think of James. That had worked splendidly in the daytime with Daphne and Aunt Marielle keeping her company, but in the nights… Poppy closed her eyes and released a soft breath.

In the nights, she dreamed of James. The memory of their kisses was always there in the shadows of her thoughts, and the desire to do more with him a constant torment and temptation. Reading that book, *A Guide to*

Passionate Romps between a Lord and his Lady, did not help. It was naughty and salacious and spoke to so many hidden desires stirring inside Poppy. In the darkness of her chamber, Poppy often found herself squeezing her thighs together, trying to quench the warm, tight ache that bloomed between them. However, what she missed the most was chatting with James.

"How have you been, Poppy?"

That gentle inquiry had her turning around. He had dropped the reins of the horses, and they grazed, drifting from them. She walked toward the lake, and James fell in beside her.

"Your sister and Aunt have been wonderful. Being here is also a calming respite from my sisters and stepmother; one I never knew I needed," she admitted with a rueful smile. "I never realized before how much of my time was taken up with doing simple errands for my sisters. Now I've had much time for myself, and I spent a great deal of it reading, playing the pianoforte, and enjoying my dance lessons. Your library is wonderful and filled with many classics."

"I am glad to hear it."

"And how have things been for you in town?"

"A dead bore."

Poppy jerked her gaze to his to find him staring at her. She choked down a chuckle before replying, "I gather you do not enjoy the social events of the season much. I recalled my sister mentioning you do not dance or socialize much at society events. Why?"

"Within society, one does not dance for the pleasure of it. At least it is better not as an unmarried gentleman. It is only seen as a signal of potential interest. I do not want to encourage anyone in vain."

"I see." Poppy searched his expression carefully. "So I gather you have not danced with my sister all week."

James scoffed, his eyes darkening with displeasure. "Not for lack of your stepmother trying. The lady is persistent, but I do not have time for games, nor do I tolerate the schemes and ridiculousness from matchmaking mamas."

This was said with an icy hardness she was not used to from him, and Poppy was entirely uncertain how to respond.

"Your sister does not lack in admirers. I am sure she will soon make a good match."

Just not with you. And Poppy's heart was extraordinarily glad to know it. "When do you return to town?"

"Tomorrow evening."

Another tight ache settled deep into her chest. "And why did you journey down this time?" Poppy knew it was for her, but she wanted him to admit his fancy. Why, she could not say, for she was sure nothing would come of it. But somehow, it mattered to her greatly.

"I fancied giving you some lessons in riding astride."

Her eyes rounded. "Riding astride?"

"Yes. I even brought down breeches and a shirt that will fit your build." His eyes traversed over her body in a thorough sweep before he looked away, his jaw tightening.

"And we are to have this lesson when?"

"Tomorrow morning."

Poppy grinned, thoroughly scandalized. "Whyever did you think I might like riding astride?"

He glanced down at her, his expression sober. She held herself still when he reached out and twined a wisp of her loose hair around one of his fingers.

"There is a certain freedom in it, more glorious than when riding sidesaddle. More control. More speed. More joy. I believe you would like that. There is something inside of you that yearns to be unrestrained and happy, and I simply thought you would love being able to ride astride."

Poppy stared up at him wordlessly, stunned that he could see so deeply into the things she felt inside but had not voiced.

"Of course, this is something you will do in the privacy of your country home."

Poppy smiled up at him and said softly, "Of course."

James tucked the strand of hair behind her ear, a profound regret gleaming in his eyes.

A perplexing weight settled inside her chest, causing an ache and her throat to tighten. *What do you regret so*, she silently asked.

They strolled for several more minutes, talking about the mundane gossips from town, each careful to not broach a too-intimate topic. That evening Poppy relaxed for an hour in her bath, allowing the water's heat to soothe away her lingering stiffness and aches in her body. She gathered that a long bath might become a nightly ritual until she became proficient in riding astride. Dinner was a scrumptious and lively feast, and afterward, she played for everyone in the music room while Daphne sang.

Now Poppy lay in her large bed, her mind unable to fall asleep. There was something different between her and James. He watched her with a puzzling mix of craving and wariness. Even at dinner, he had been reserved to the point of stiffness, but only with her. A situation even Daphne and Aunt Marielle seemed aware of, for they had shared speaking glances Poppy did not understand. However, whenever her eyes and James's gaze collided, the burning hunger she saw there robbed her of breath and her wits.

He wanted her. She was sure of it. Then she recalled his desire to not marry as yet. What ambition did he own why he was determined to wait years to settle down? Poppy was quite aware such luxury was only the purview of gentlemen.

What if I should wait on you, James?

The question seemed to come from outside of herself, and Poppy gasped, lurching to sit upright in bed. *Rubbish*, her common sense cried. *Wait on him?* A man is always wanted, regardless of age. At the same time, after a few more years of waiting, Poppy would be considered extremely ineligible—a decrepit spinster in the last bloom of youth—to be acceptable as anyone's wife, especially not that of an earl.

"Do not start having silly and foolish hopes," she whispered in the darkness of the chamber before snuggling down and falling into a deep sleep, still with those hopes burrowing even deeper inside her heart.

CHAPTER 10

The following morning, Poppy rose from her restless slumber, eager to visit the stables and ride for the day. She was naughtily clad in breeches that revealed every curve of her body and a shirt that thankfully covered her rump. Daphne had choked on her tea when she spied Poppy, but Aunt Marielle had only harrumphed. Meeting James by the stables, admiration lit in his eyes when he spied her. Poppy hid her grin when she noted the flush on his sharply defined cheekbones.

"Let's get to riding," James called.

Her mare was led out by Fernley, who winked at her. Poppy smiled, and with the aid of James and the mounting block, seated her horse astride. It felt different. Oddly more intimidating. She gently gathered the reins and relaxed under James' instructions, following the back-and-forth movement of the horse. Poppy rocked with her mare's stride, easing into the familiarity of riding astride. She could feel the bunch of muscles and the power of the horse beneath her. She ran her gloved hand through the coarse hair of the horse's mane. Her mare's ears were pricked, telling Poppy she was ready, but waiting.

"Lean forward slightly," James said from beside her.

Poppy complied, and immediately her horse nudged forward into a steady lope. The urge to go faster beat in her heart, but she restrained the need bubbling inside her, desperate to spew out. They trotted gently along the lanes, and Poppy stared into the distance, a peculiar sadness upon her.

"James," she said, glancing over at him, "Do you ever feel this frantic longing inside for something…*more*. You do not know what it is really, but the shadows of the feelings are there inside you, straining and reaching. And it is so frustrating because you do not understand fully what you so desperately want."

"Yes," he said gruffly, careful in not looking at her.

"What do you do then when such sensations play havoc with your peace of mind?"

For a long time, he did not answer. Then he turned and held her eyes fiercely with his.

"What do you want, Poppy?"

His intensity shook her. *You. More kisses with you. More laughter. More dancing. More of everything.* But she did not say that. "I wish I could go faster; feel the wind on my face."

"You are several lessons away from that, I am afraid. I have no wish for you to fall and break your pretty neck." Yet he indicated for her to draw the horse to a stop. James dismounted, helped Poppy from her horse and placed her atop his. Then to Poppy's shocked delight, he mounted behind her.

The feel of his body behind her was nerve-wracking.

"Hold the reins as well, loosely, and lean forward slightly. We are going to go fast."

Her heart in her throat, Poppy nodded.

At James's urging, each stride of his stallion gained momentum until the horse flattened his ears and hurtled onward. The ground rushed past at astonishing speed, and Poppy laughed, feeling breathless. As if the stallion picked up on her delight, Poppy felt the shift of the stallion beneath her, the great muscles working beneath him as his strides lengthened. The ground raced by alarmingly fast, but Poppy's eyes were on the endless meadows before them, the blue of the sky, the feel of James behind her.

The hoofbeats filled her ears, blocking all noise except the wind…the glorious rushing wind. The power and speed were exhilarating and even terrifying.

James slowed them and eased the horse until he stopped. Laughing shakily, Poppy turned and glanced up at his face. He was grinning, his hair windswept.

"Now, how was that?" he murmured.

"I felt like I would have taken flight. James, that was glorious, thank you!" Then Poppy leaned in and brushed a kiss against his mouth.

James faltered into stillness as if this were the first they were kissing. Poppy drew back embarrassed, for she had not thought about it; only her exuberance and impetuosity had pushed her to kiss him. "James, I…"

Her words petered out at the look in his eyes—such burning hunger and also caution. He shook his head as if dazed. Then his chest lifted on a savage breath. With her own dazed sense of awe, she noted one of the gloved hands on his thigh shook before he clenched it into a tight fist. It occurred to Poppy then that whenever James kissed her, he felt *extraordinary* things, and he had to be careful, or he feared he would seduce her.

Poppy smiled, wanting to hug and squeeze him. That a man as handsome and sought after could want her so much was remarkable. She turned around because she did not want him to see the wide smile curving her mouth. He did not mention her enthusiastic and very chaste kiss. They only rode back to collect her mare and then headed to the manor in silence; an odd sort of tension filled with so many unspoken questions and longing brewing between them.

༺☙༻

POPPY WOKE EARLY the next day, knowing James would already be gone. He had not departed yesterday evening but had stayed one more night to dine with them. With an indelicate yawn, Poppy pushed from the bed. After quickly finishing her morning ablutions with the assistance of Daphne's lady's maid, Poppy made her way to the breakfast room. Only Aunt Marielle was there and informed Poppy James had departed for town at the crack of dawn.

Poppy went to the sideboard laden with food and filled her plate with succulent ham, eggs, kippers. There was also porridge and cold meats, but she ignored those, selecting a few pieces of toast.

Daphne entered the breakfast room just as Poppy sat and started eating. They grinned at each other, and

Daphne hurriedly filled her plate before sitting in front of Poppy.

"I received a letter from mama. She says we are to return to town for Lady Bloomfield's ball, which is in a few days," Daphne said. "The countess's ball is immensely popular, and mama believes it a great opportunity for you. Mama, however, will not be in town when we arrive. She is to visit Cousin Euphemia in Derbyshire, who is about to give birth to her first child, and so will stay for a few weeks."

A thrill of excitement went through Poppy at the thought of seeing James again so soon. With a frown, she mentally stomped on the sensation until it died. "Then we are to leave this afternoon?"

Daphne grinned. "Yes. I daresay we will pack and depart right after breakfast. Are you to accompany us to town, Aunt Marielle, since mama will be gone?"

"I will be returning to Bath. Perhaps tomorrow, my dears. I am exceedingly tired of town life. Too much excitement."

"Please, Aunt Marielle," Daphne pleaded.

Her aunt smiled. "Fine. I might be persuaded to visit for a few days."

They laughed and hurriedly finished their breakfast to start their packing.

THE POPPY ASHFORD who drove back to town with Lady Daphne was much more confident in her demeanor and felt the veneer of sophistication she had acquired would stand her in good stead against the vagaries of society.

Instead of returning to her stepmother's townhouse, they arrived at Lady Daphne's much grander one. Aunt Marielle accompanied them, and a second carriage followed with the servants and luggage.

James awaited their arrival and greeted them as they entered the elegant townhouse in Russell Square.

"Welcome back, Daphne, Aunt and Miss Ashford," he said, smiling. "Were there any problems with the journey?"

He kissed his sister and aunt but merely bowed to Poppy. Yet his eyes lingered discreetly on her, sweeping from her head to toes. Then the dratted man winked. A sweet feeling brushed against her heart. Poppy grinned and swept him an elegant curtsy in return.

"James, everything went smooth as clockwork, thanks to your excellent organization and staff," Daphne said, removing her bonnet.

"We have some business matters to attend to," James said. "I will be in the study awaiting you."

"I will just show Poppy to her room, and I will be back down to talk to you, brother."

Poppy wondered what her stepmother would think about her being welcomed into society under Lady Daphne's and the countess's aegis. It would not reflect well on her stepmother's treatment of her if Poppy were brought out by an unrelated family. Still, she was not going to complain, because she had been happier in Lady Daphne's and James's company than she had been since Richard's death.

Poppy realized that she could not completely avoid her stepmother and half-sisters but feared that it would not be a pleasant experience, especially if they saw that she was well-received by society. While in the country, she had been able to push their contempt from her mind, but now she recalled their disagreeableness to her.

With an internal sigh, she followed Lady Daphne upstairs and was shown into a pretty room decorated in lilac with the soft furnishings in deep purple and gold. A fire had already been lit as the weather was surprisingly chilly for late spring. A young maid bobbed a curtsy and took her bandbox, which Poppy had brought with her. Footmen followed, carrying up her luggage. She had only taken one case with her to the country, but another case with the earl's coat of arms had been borrowed to transport her new wardrobe.

Poppy could not imagine how she would ever repay their great kindness.

"Poppy, this is Amy, who has been asked to act as your maid for your stay with us in town," Daphne informed her, kissing her cheek. "If you could get freshened up and changed, we have lots to do. I'll meet you downstairs."

Daphne floated off while Amy hurried to bring hot water and prepare her new mistress. Half an hour later, Amy was laying out a charming evening dress in a pale blue. The gown was in watered silk with faint stripes in the weave. The skirt was plain but very gathered, the bodice ornamented with the silk piped in three lines from the dropped shoulders to the front point of the waist. The short sleeves were puffed and ended in three ruffles of a slightly darker blue lace, and the same lace edged the neckline. Poppy marveled at the material which would reflect the light as it moved with the wearer.

Poppy touched the elegant garment. "Amy, where is this dress from? It is not one of mine…"

"Her Ladyship ordered it with the other gowns in your wardrobe. Such pretty gowns—you are so very lucky, Miss. I will unpack and press your other gowns once I have got you ready, Miss."

And there were even more new gowns, shoes, and assorted unmentionables awaiting her here. No doubt James's doing. Poppy allowed Amy to help her into the gown and to arrange her hair.

"It is so easy to curl your hair, Miss; you have such beautiful hair, so few ladies have real natural curls," Amy gushed. "I do not even need to use hair pads to make the new styles."

Poppy stared at herself in the cheval mirror, quite surprised at how pretty she appeared. Her hair had been caught up in an elegant chignon with several artful tendrils about her forehead. "Thank you, Amy. You have done a beautiful job with it. I suppose I should go down. It is early for dinner, but Lady Daphne suggested we had things to do. Do you know where I could find her?"

"I believe Lady Daphne is in the baroque drawing-room; it is the second door on the left at the bottom of the stairs, Miss."

Poppy descended and found the correct door. She knocked and was bid to enter.

Daphne and James were already present and consuming a glass of sherry and some fancy cakes, which had been arranged on a small table.

"Come in, Poppy. James and I have been discussing which of these invitations we should accept. I think that

Lady Sanders's musicale might be the right event for us to attend first," Daphne said, smiling widely.

"I don't know any of these people," Poppy said, glancing at the pile of invitations. "I will be happy to attend anything you think might be suitable, Lady Daphne."

Surprised eyes met hers. "Why so formal, Poppy? We are not in company. Would you like a glass of sherry and some of these cakes? Our cook has some fancy notions which mama and I tolerate, but his confectionary skills are superior."

Daphne poured her a glass and handed her a plate with a selection of cakes. Poppy's mouth watered with anticipation. It looked like this particular cook would be someone she could happily emulate. The pastel-colored macaroons were delicious, and the confections made with coconut and flavored with rum were the best she had ever tasted.

"Daphne, I received many invitations while you and Poppy were in the country. I have only accepted the Childers' ball so far, but I thought you might be able to select which ones would be best for Miss Poppy to attend," James said, handing over another sheaf of invitations. "We want the ones where respectable and notable gentlemen who are considering marriage will attend."

Poppy smiled at his encouraging wink, but there was a heavy ache inside her belly. It was also an entirely unpleasant sensation, not the sweet flutters when he smiled at her. She had developed such complex feelings for James; Poppy did not feel there was room inside her heart for someone else at the moment. However, all of this he was doing was for her to find a suitor, marry, and live a happy life.

How could she disappoint all of his expectations and Daphne's effort? More urgently, how did she stop herself from falling hopelessly in love with James?

CHAPTER 11

Over the next few days, Poppy was kept busy. There was shopping, and more shopping, visits to the museums—something she had always hoped to be allowed, but her stepmother had despised such activities. Then there was a trip to the theatre where she saw the melodrama *Old Heads and Young Hearts*, written and starring the famed Irish actor and playwright Dion Boucicault.

Daphne informed her that his real given name was Dionysius Lardner "Dion" Boucicault which Poppy thought amusing and could understand why he had shortened his first name. Many callers visited and amiably conversed with her and Daphne, and so far, Poppy had managed to avoid catching sight of her stepmother or her sisters. That was a relief to Poppy as the many people to whom she had been introduced had all welcomed her and issued further invitations in the hopes that she would appear at their events.

Tonight was to be the night of Lady Sanders' musicale. Poppy was nervous, but at least she knew her skills on the pianoforte were more than adequate. It was not performing that she was concerned about. Daphne had told Poppy that her stepmother and sisters had also been invited and had indicated they would attend.

Poppy anticipated the cutting remarks her family might make, especially if James attended and paid her any attention. Which according to his plan to make her appear eligible, his attention was a necessity. If her stepmother had her cap still set for James as her son-in-law, the entire night might get ugly. With a silent groan, Poppy dismissed such worries.

Amy laid out a new gown in bronze crepe, decorated with tiny cream silk roses. A spray of cream roses had been specially created to pin into Poppy's luxuriant black hair. A beautiful cream silk shawl embroidered in bronze and gold had been purchased to complement the gown.

She took a deep breath in and straightened her back. Poppy examined her appearance in the mirror. It was amazing the difference fine clothes and a frivolous coiffure could make. She looked rather pretty and elegant. Poppy thanked Amy for her assistance and descended to the entrance hall. Aunt Marielle was already waiting, but Daphne was not yet down. They waited a few minutes as Aunt Marielle reassured her that she would be the best pianist there and inquiring about what she intended to play.

"I was thinking of playing one of Chopin's études and something from Mendelssohn, but if they want me to play for the dancing, I have learned some of the latest Johann Strauss's waltzes."

Aunt Marielle's expression brightened. "Whatever you

play, I am sure it will be wonderful. James is to meet us there, and I believe he is bringing Lord Worsley with him."

Poppy frowned. "Lord Worsley?"

"A disreputable one that, but he is recently married and violently in love with his wife and uncaring that society is aware of it."

Poppy laughed. "I shall look forward to making his acquaintance."

Aunt Marielle sniffed. "It is not like Worsley to attend musicales. Perhaps my nephew twisted his arm a little."

Then just as the carriage had been drawn around, Daphne dashed down the stairs wearing a lovely, deep wine gown trimmed with golden ribbons. It was fussier than Poppy's gown, having several deep-layered frills to the skirt, but Daphne had suggested that simpler styles would flatter Poppy more as deep frills would accentuate her lack of inches in height.

They were handed into the carriage, and they set off for the short journey to Lord and Lady Sanders's home. They were still relatively early. Half a dozen carriages were queuing to disembark their passengers. Still, according to Daphne, many more would be expected, although Lady Sanders had disclosed that it was to be a small, select gathering.

"The last event that Lady Sanders said would be small, admitted at least three hundred people, Poppy, so do not expect it *not* to be a crush! I am glad that we indicated that you would be prepared to play when we accepted the invitation because I suspect the organization will be challenging and that those who expect to be slotted into the program last minute will be unable to perform," Daphne said, smiling and looking around.

Poppy leaned closer to Daphne and said, "I think the largest group I have ever performed for was about fifty, and that was for a country dance in the village after one Clarence Withers *finally* married Abigail Cubbins, which as she had borne him two children already out of wedlock was an event much anticipated."

Daphne gasped. "Already out of wedlock? The scandal."

Poppy chuckled, enjoying just chatting with Daphne. A friendship was forming between them, and Poppy, at times, wanted to hug her. She'd had so few friends in her life. Everyone Poppy had gotten close to in the village, her stepmother had disapproved of the association. "Very much so. We were all thrilled when he came up to scratch. I think almost everyone was in their cups after I had played the first three dances."

"Oh, you must have been frightened…"

"Not really…I had known most of them all my life, and they treated me like Dresden porcelain. Old Preacher Calvin Hobson escorted me to the hall and back and watched over me the whole time. It was at his urging that I played, although the village band played too. I think they were more to be praised for their determination than their skill at playing. I concluded that one of the fiddlers was playing a completely different tune in counterpoint to the main one for some of the time," Poppy said, laughing.

Daphne tried to suppress a burst of laughter, but Aunt Marielle made no such attempt, doubling up and then having to wipe her eyes with her handkerchief. The carriage pulled forward and now only had one carriage ahead of them. That carriage, however, disgorged Lord and Lady Hayes, Rebecca, and Mrs. Ashford.

Poppy leaned back from the carriage window, not wanting to have them spot her and have to make conversation with them. She could not bear their spiteful tongues and nasty remarks. Not yet. However, neither of her sisters or stepmother looked back as they strolled up to the front door of the mansion.

"I was hoping they would cry off," Poppy said with a sigh.

"Courage, Poppy. We will stare them down. You have every right to be here, and if your stepmother had any family decency, she would have brought you out years ago," Daphne said tersely, revealing her partisanship for Poppy's cause.

It was a warm night, so no coats had been worn, as it was not a formal ball. No receiving line was held, but waiters were distributing glasses of some fine white wine, which the ladies accepted. James was waiting, looking very handsome, in the entrance hall. His bronze brocade waistcoat almost matched Poppy's gown, which she thought a favorable augury or coincidence. She did wonder as she smiled and curtsied to him whether it had been deliberate on his part.

"Daphne, you look delightful as usual," James said to his sister. "Aunt Marielle, that is a stunning new gown… very imperial."

Aunt Marielle had chosen to dress in rich purple and wore a hair ornament that displayed some fine amethysts and pearls in her steel-grey hair. But while he spoke, his eyes were eating up Poppy's appearance. Poppy thought James looked a little uncomfortable as if his normal unruffled demeanor had been unsettled by something. James continued, bowing over her hand. "Miss Ashford, you look simply stunning."

Warmth flowered throughout her body at the sincerity in his tone and the measured way he stared at her. As if he could not help himself. As if he wanted to say more but did not dare.

James waved his hand to a handsome gentleman standing by his side. "May I introduce you to Viscount Worsley, a good friend of mine. Do not let him lead you astray."

Poppy frowned slightly, recalling the rules of etiquette Daphne and Aunt Marielle had painstakingly mentioned. She smiled when she realized what was amiss. "My lord, you know perfectly well that you should have introduced Lord Worsley to me, as his importance is far elevated above mine."

"I am honored to make your acquaintance, Miss Ashford, and my rank defers to your beauty," Worsley said, bowing flamboyantly over her hand, his silver-gray eyes glittering with humor.

James rolled his eyes, and Poppy swallowed her laugh. Lord Worsley offered Poppy his arm, and James walked between his relations. They headed into a grand ballroom that had been set with rows of chairs for the musicale. There were also stands and chairs set for an orchestra, a grand piano, and a full-size harp.

Lady Sanders bustled over, and James made the introduction to Poppy, this time correctly. Poppy took in the full glory of Lady Sanders, who was a lady of about sixty years of age. Her hair was white and severely restrained but topped by a small tiara of fine diamonds. Their hostess wore a dark pink gown of which the skirt had several scalloped flounces which were edged dramatically in scarlet. She creaked and wheezed a little as she moved and wafted with an overpowering perfume that contained many floral scents.

In her hand, Lady Sanders held a slightly crumpled list and a pencil dangled from her wrist, and she crossed off Poppy's name, which indicated that she was to play fifth.

"Very pleased to meet you, Miss Ashford. I have heard great things of your playing."

Poppy jolted and sent a swift glance at James, who widened his eyes innocently.

"I do not think you will have much competition from the earlier performances," Lady Sanders continued. "I try to encourage some of the younger generations, but I put the less talented on first before the hall has filled up, then try to scatter the real musicians through the program to leaven the dough, so to speak. Now, Kingsley, you have failed to volunteer, and you have such a beautiful voice. Can I persuade you to entertain us later in the evening?"

Poppy glanced at him. James sang?

"I have been so busy with the estate's affairs, and I have not practiced anything in a long time. You have a long list; I beg to be excused," James said politely but with a great deal of charm. "I also have a matter to speak about with Worsley…"

James's scowl blackened, and Poppy had to look away before her laughter escaped. Poppy had no notion where

Worsley had vanished to, but James could not use anything with his friend as an excuse.

Lady Sanders harrumphed. "You know perfectly well, young man, that this is a great opportunity for me. You have not attended any musicale in years, and now you are at mine. A triumph! There will be an outcry if you do not sing at least the Elf King. Do you think you could play the accompaniment to that, Miss Ashford? I have the music if you need it; most of the pianists here would not be up to the mark for playing so difficult a piece. What are you planning on playing, by the way?"

Poppy hid her smile at James's consternation. "I was thinking of a Chopin étude and possibly a piece by Mendelssohn, but I know the Elf King and can play it with the music. It has been a while since I played it, but it was one of my brother's favorites."

"Excellent! Well, that's all organized. You have an accompanist, and I, for one, will accept no excuses. I will have the music found and sent over so you can remind yourself of the music Kingsley will sing."

Lady Sanders moved on to the next guests, and James turned to Poppy.

"You sing?" she asked, staring up at him.

"Like a frog. I cannot imagine why she would want to subject her guests."

Poppy smiled. "I am certain it is nothing of the sort, or Lady Sanders would not have trapped you so thoroughly."

There was a look she could not decipher as he stared down at her.

"Do you really not mind playing for me? The Elf King is a bit of a stinker with all those rumbling broken chords."

Poppy chuckled, amused with his droll wit. "I rather like it, although it does need a good singer to maintain all that histrionic dread. It is easier to play than Chopin. I suspect he must have had giant hands to make all the stretches."

James nodded, scanning the crowd. "His portraits do suggest that he had beautiful hands. I wish I had been able to hear him in person. I believe he still performs in Paris occasionally."

The ballroom was quickly filling up, and although Poppy could see where her family was seated in the second row of the sitting arrangements, they took no notice of her or James and his family. The longer that debacle could be postponed, the better, in her opinion.

A gentleman she assumed was Lord Sanders climbed the dais and announced, "Ladies and gentlemen, would you please find your seats; the performances are about to begin."

Daphne's party sat toward the rear of the ballroom and settled down to listen to the first performers. Poppy was painfully aware that James sat beside her. Every shift, even if a slight one, felt as if heat rippled through her. Did he feel it too, this connection between them? Or was it all Poppy's imagination?

More glasses of wine were being handed around as a trio of three girls ascended the dais. One seated herself with her music at the piano, and the others clustered around. The seated audience were still gossiping amongst themselves, but Lord Sanders glared at everyone and struck his cane on the floor to silence them.

Poppy noticed that the three girls were similar in

appearance and suspected they were sisters. The girl at the piano played and sang a traditional song and her sisters sang along with her. Poppy thought they were lovely and did well despite their apparent nervousness. The three sisters were revealed as the Misses Jepson when Lord Sanders thanked them for their efforts. There was a brief round of applause, although it was louder in one quarter of the ballroom where family or friends showed some partiality.

The second performer was an ethereal blonde, dressed in ivory satin. She floated across the dais to the harp and seated herself behind it. Beautiful notes rippled from the strings in harmony and seemed to vaguely describe a melody. Her performance was at least not painful to the ears; however, as her piece continued, it was clear the young lady's sense of rhythm was erratic. Beyond the approximate selection of the strings lacked any real understanding of the music itself. By the end of the piece, Poppy was anxious for her and thought she acquitted herself pleasantly.

One young buck stood and scandalously called out, "Bellissima!" and blew kisses to the blonde.

The announcement for the third performer was given after the blonde, Lady Lucinda, had curtsied herself off. Poppy started as she realized the next performer was to be her sister. She looked radiant in a pale blue gown, but Poppy found herself anxious as Rebecca sat down at the piano.

Poppy charitably prayed that her sister would perform well. As Rebecca began to play, a hush fell over the audience, then several of the matrons snapped their fans open and noisily fluttered them in front of their noses. Poppy glanced around the room. Some people were sitting stoically with pained expressions on their faces, others were wrestling with the desire not to laugh, some even whispered in their neighbors' ears. Then Poppy noticed that several of the younger men were looking around and studying the ladies, and at least two were staring directly at her. Poppy wondered why, because she doubted many would recognize her as Rebecca's half-sister; they simply did not look alike.

"You are nervous," James murmured.

"Yes…I…" Poppy smiled ruefully. "I want her to do well."

"Have I ever told you that you are an amazing person?"

She cast him a quick, startled glance.

"Sometime last week when your stepmother tried to convince me to dance with your lovely sister, Mrs. Ashford spent a remarkable amount of time highlighting your nonexistent charm and skills. Yet here you are so earnestly wanting her to do well when she would have the opposite thoughts for you."

"Shh, she's my half-sister, and despite everything, I do love her and hope for her dreams to come true," Poppy finally said as Rebecca stood to curtsy to the crowd.

The applause was very muted, and it was only when Rebecca realized how little applause she was receiving that her face flushed in chagrin. Then her eyes fell directly on Poppy, clapping and sitting beside James. A look of pure shock stole over her features before quickly being replaced with one of fury.

Poppy gasped to see her sister glaring at her so. Rebecca fled the stage and out of the ballroom, sobbing. Poppy considered going after her sister to comfort her, but decided such overtures would not be welcomed, and she was to play after the next performance.

The next performer was a young man with a florid complexion and carroty hair, and he was accompanied by an older woman who was clearly his accompanist. She looked like a governess of some sort. Her playing was correct and accomplished. She played the introduction to a medley of nautical airs, which the young gentleman sang out in a jolly, warbling tenor, ending with Arne's Rule Britannia, which received rousing cheers from a group of his cronies and considerable applause.

"You are up next," James said. "Are you still nervous?"

"No," Poppy whispered. Such a fib. This was her very first musicale, and she was not only an observer but a participant. "Perhaps a tiny bit anxious."

"You will do beautifully," he said with such calm assurance and confidence Poppy relaxed. She also saw the heart-rending tenderness of his gaze.

Poppy stood up and strolled up the side aisle to the steps to the piano. She waited for the young man's bow and thanks to end before taking her place at the piano. Poppy turned and gazed at the audience and smiled. Her glance swept past the faces of her furious stepmother and the obviously incensed Lavinia and back to where James sat waiting for her to begin.

The dratted man winked, and Poppy briefly looked away so she would not grin like a silly goose. She would ignore the rest and play only for him. Poppy breathed deeply and let her fingers pull the music from the keys of the instrument in front of her. Then she was lost in the melodies of Chopin as the crowd sat silently, letting the sound reach deep into their shallow souls. As she played the finale, she paused and glanced at Lord Sanders, unsure whether she should play her second piece or perhaps make her curtsy and retire. As the last notes melted away, the applause thundered through the room. "Encore, encore," was yelled, and the clapping went on.

She stood and curtsied, then looked to Lord Sanders.

He banged his cane once more, "Superb, magnificent, Miss Ashford. Please honor us with another piece..."

So, Poppy sat back down and played the lyrical romantic strains of Mendelssohn to an audience enthralled by the beauty of the music. Once more, she reached the final flourishes and allowed the notes to flow through her to the end. Then she stood and curtsied and descended from the dais to another eruption of applause and demands for "More, more!"

As Poppy passed her stepmother and Lavinia to return to her seat, she noticed their faces contorted in their anger. They would never forgive her for it and would surely blame Poppy for Rebecca's earlier mortification. There were several more acts before the summons for James to perform. Schubert's Erlkönig, or the Elf King, was a settling of Goethe's poem, while normally performed by a soprano, it was apparently James' tour de force.

Poppy was unsure whether she should change the key or not, from the rumbling minor bass telling the haunting tale of the wicked Elf King and a terrified child. James produced a mellow baritone which he modulated to fit the eerie tale. He moved and acted out the story, sending chills running up and down the spines of his watchers. His voice might not have had the full power of an opera soloist, but his performance was powerful and moving. His applause was brilliant, and Poppy joined the crowd in their applause.

The rest of the evening proved magical and exhausting. Poppy met so many people who effusively complimented her playing, and then invited her to join their party another time for some rout or picnic. By the time supper arrived, she wanted to sleep, and laughingly told James so. They did not linger long after, and within an hour, Poppy was in her bed, mightily exhausted and staring at the ceiling.

"Today was another wonderful experience," she murmured in the dark. "And I am another step closer to attaining everything I've ever wanted." *A husband, children, to be mistress in my own home.*

Except as she rolled over and sank in deep slumber, it was not this phantom *beau* that stole into her dreams, but James—laughing and dancing, then her kissing his lovely, laughing mouth.

CHAPTER 12

The very next evening, Poppy attended Lady Bloomfield's most anticipated ball with Daphne. The ballroom was tastefully decorated in white, gold and touches of crimson. The drapes over the huge front windows were crimson velvet with golden tassels. The ballroom, which extended the full depth of the house, was glazed at the other end with the drapes left unclosed, opening into the small but exquisite gardens behind the mansion.

The crush was already stifling, and Poppy yearned to sneak outside into that garden for a breath of fresh air. While the season was exciting, it could also be exhausting. It astonished Poppy that some attended an event, or more than one event, every day. It also amazed her how many people from the musicale were in attendance, and they greeted her warmly and sometimes with overt enthusiasm. Even the hostess begged her to come to her own musicale next week and play for her guests.

"You are so very lovely tonight," Daphne said, smiling.

Poppy wore another of her new gowns—this one rose-colored with a scalloped neckline. It flattered her figure remarkably, and she wore the pearls she had inherited from her mother. Her hair had been caught up in a cascade of curls and was unadorned with flowers or jewelry. Yet many admiring glances settled on her by several gentlemen.

Daphne was delighted, while Poppy was…she swallowed. She was not entirely certain what she felt at the moment.

"I see my sisters and stepmother are in attendance. I will go and greet them."

Daphne frowned. "Are you certain?"

"Yes. I dread a confrontation with them because it can be exhausting. And I must return home eventually. I cannot stay under your roof until I am married."

"Yes, you can."

Poppy laughed. "My dear, Daphne, that would cast too many shadows on me and my family's relationship. The tongues will wag for certain."

Poppy was also concerned about Rebecca. Though she stood beside her mother and sister, appearing resplendent in a lime green gown, there was an air of melancholy about her. Poppy made her way over, and Lavinia spied her first and uncurled her fan.

"Poppy, dearest, you are back in town and importuning Lady Daphne. People might start to wonder if you have a home," Lavinia said with biting malice.

Poppy dipped into a slight curtsy and smiled serenely. "It was mother who taught me it was dreadfully impolite to refuse an earnestly-pressed invitation. Surely you would not want me to act poorly and refuse Lady Daphne's kindness." She looked at Rebecca, who had taken on a mulish expression. "How are you, Rebecca?"

"As if you cared," she spat. "You deliberately played at Lady Sanders's musicale even though you knew I would be one of the performers."

Poppy sighed. "Do not be ridiculous. My playing has nothing to do with your capabilities. I do not like when you prattle nonsense as if you are not a lovely girl with charm and her own sense of self."

"How dare you lecture your sister," her stepmother sniffed. "And she is not incorrect. It is Rebecca's time to shine, and you are a spiteful thing to try and steal her spotlight, given everything we have done for you."

Lavinia stepped forward. "Do you know how mortifying it is to see you strolling about in your borrowed finery as if you are a debutante? If you had any hopes of receiving a pound from us for being Rebecca's chaperone, you are mistaken!"

Poppy stared at her family, wondering if they could really be this horribly obtuse and petty. "Rebecca has everything. A great beauty, a lovely charm, and a dowry, yet you are jealous of the little I have accomplished. How ridiculous you all are."

Lavinia gasped as if she could not believe Poppy's temerity. She did not wait for a reply but turned away from her family, confident they would not start a scene here.

The dancing started, and Poppy gave herself up to enjoyment. She danced at least three sets of the polka and was laughing breathlessly when James approached her. A ripple went through the crowd, and Poppy flushed, her fingers gripping the edges of her gown.

He bowed and held out his hand. "I have it on the highest authority a waltz will now be played. Will you do me the honor, Miss Ashford?"

Once again, she felt the eyes of assembled guests upon them. Poppy laid her hand in his and allowed him to take her onto the dance floor. She peered up at him as they took their positions with the rest of the dancers. Just being held in his arms was sinfully delicious.

"I did not think you would come. Daphne said you sent a message apologizing for your inability to attend, for you would be buried in your study, working."

"Some investment returns," he returned mildly, placing his hand by her elbow.

"You do that a lot."

At his quizzical glance, she clarified. "Many times, your absence is apologized away due to you having to work. Why?"

His eyes darkened, and for a moment, she thought he would not answer. "Several of my estates are still in the red."

Poppy stared at him in shock. "In the red…in debt?"

"Yes. They have been for several years. Before my father died."

"Oh, James, how could you have offered me a dowry when—"

"Poppy, your dowry is just a penny. Do not worry about it."

A penny? Ten thousand pounds was just a penny? She glared at him. The chords of the waltz were struck, and the beautiful notes danced in the air. Poppy found her hand trembling and tried to still it.

"Are you afraid you are still not good at dancing?"

It was the idea of being in his arms, of feeling the weight of his hand on her waist. Just being this close had a terrible effect on her senses. "If I had any such apprehension, I would have most firmly rejected your offer to dance," she said with disarming candor. "I shall do my best not to step on your toes."

James smiled, and then he swept her away in the beautiful and intricate dance. They soared and twirled together for several minutes, lost in the beauty of the music and being in each other's arms.

"Many gentlemen are looking at you with longing," James said, an odd tightness about his mouth. "I declare our campaign a success. Once I release you, they will flock to your side, and you will have your pick of them. Dance away the night until your feet tire."

"And what will you do?"

"Return home to my investment report."

"You only came to dance with me?"

"Yes."

Every time his gaze met hers, Poppy's heart turned over in response. "To place the finishing touches on your master plan or because you had to come?"

Something intense flared through his eyes. "I came because I wanted to dance with you. It is only a perfect coincidence it is the icing needed for our plans," he responded with perfect gravity.

His lack of charming flirtation told Poppy he did not enjoy the reason he came. James did not like wanting her.

After coming back to him in a twirl, she asked, "Why must you wait three years to marry?"

His head snapped back before his expression smoothed. "Because I made an oath to do so."

"You made an oath not to marry until three years?"

"Yes."

"And you must honor this promise?"

"Yes."

His tone was implacable.

"What if…" A lump grew in her throat, and she stared up at him, unable to finish her thoughts as he glided her in several intricate steps.

"What if what, Poppy?"

"What if you should fall in love before the three years?"

Poppy never imagined eyes could burn with such passion.

"It is unlikely I will ever fall in love," he finally said, his eyes dark with unfathomable emotions. "I cannot afford such sentiments, nor do I hunger for them."

A piercing anguish she had never felt before ripped throughout her entire body. *It was all one-sided*. She struggled for equanimity, grateful she had not done anything as silly as telling him of her feelings.

The dance ended, and he bowed to her. "I must take my leave, and I wish you every success going forward."

"James," she breathed softly, hating how her heart beat. "Why does that sound like a goodbye?"

A soft smile touched his mouth before he turned away and melted through the crush. The rest of the night passed in a blur of dancing and laughing, but Poppy was painfully aware that none of it touched her real heart.

"There is a gentleman here to call upon you, Miss Poppy," the butler said, frightening a decade from Poppy's life.

With as much dignity one could muster, she straightened from the keyhole of the door. She had received a letter from her stepmother this morning requesting Poppy to call at Lavinia's home. Upon arrival, Poppy had been shown to the drawing-room, which held dozens of bouquets of flowers. All delivered for her. Her stepmother had affected a pleasant countenance and had seemed pleased for Poppy. So had Lavinia. Poppy had then realized they wanted her to marry and off their hands, or better away from the Earl of Kingsley.

They were so transparent in their plotting she had rolled her eyes. For the first time in years, Poppy believed their words and actions had lost the power to wound her. Still, it would not do for Lavinia's butler to report to his mistress that he had caught her sister eavesdropping.

"There is an explanation for my behavior which might seem rather odd and improper to you."

He cleared his throat. "I am owed no explanation, Miss Poppy, but I do understand you were eavesdropping."

She grinned up at him sheepishly. "It is that weird man, Mr. Gilford. He danced with me twice last night but barely conversed with me. Then he showed up here today with the demand to speak with the baron about grave matters that concern our future together. The sheer nerve of the man."

Humor lit in the butler's eyes. "And did you find out anything pertinent, Miss Poppy?"

She lifted a finger and wagged it. "He wishes to marry me. I cannot conceive that he would ask Lord Hayes about that matter since I would be joined with him until death parts us. Clearly, my opinion does not matter. Who would marry such a man?"

The butler looked nonplussed and offered no reply.

Poppy cleared her throat. "You said there was another gentleman?"

"Yes, one Lord Fairfax."

Poppy's heart jolted. "Viscount Fairfax?"

"Yes."

"And he asked to call upon me and not Miss Rebecca?"

"Yes."

Oh! "Has my stepmother received him?"

"Mrs. Ashford is resting. A migraine. And Lady Hayes has not yet returned from her outing, Miss Poppy."

Poppy took a steady breath and made her way to the smaller parlor where the handsome and quite charming viscount waited. His hands were perfectly clasped behind his back, his broad shoulders relaxed as he stood by the windows staring at some birds perched on a small shrub.

He turned at her entrance, and Poppy was taken aback by the smile that lit his face upon seeing her. She had only danced with him…once or twice…no, it was precisely three times. With another painful jolt of her heart, she realized the viscount had asked her to dance at almost every ball they encountered each other since her return to town.

Good heavens, has he been courting me?

It astonished Poppy that she had never considered it

before. She had simply thought him pleasant, quite good-natured, and a most charming conversationalist.

"Lord Fairfax," she greeted him, dipping into a curtsy. "What an unexpected surprise, my lord."

"Is it?" he asked with a smile and a decided twinkle in his light green eyes.

Poppy thought his smile was particularly fatuous. He walked over to her, and it was the first time she had noticed the flecks of gold at the center of his eyes. Those very eyes stared at her with too much warmth.

Bloody hell. It felt good to curse, even if silently.

A few months ago, she had no suitors, and today she had one man presumably asking for permission to marry her now, another one with courting intentions…and another one she was falling in love with, but he did not believe in sentiments.

"Ah…yes."

"I would like to invite you to a carriage ride in Hyde Park, Miss Ashford."

Poppy took a deep breath. It was best to be truthful from the get-go. "My lord, if you will permit me to be frank and honest with you?"

"I would have it no other way, Miss Ashford."

"I am excessively flattered. I cannot express how much, but I…I am not interested." Poppy winced at how badly that was done. "Forgive me, I do not wish to let you hope in vain, so I must confess that my affections are engaged elsewhere."

An arrested look appeared on the viscount's face. "Ah, with Lord Kingsley. He has made it known to all who are watching that you are indeed special. Surely it does not escape your attention that he has not made an offer, nor is he really courting you."

"I do not believe I said it was the earl." Poppy smiled politely. "Thank you for calling, Lord Fairfax, if you will excuse me." She whirled around and escaped the drawing-room. Another social gaffe on her part possibly, but she could not care at the moment.

Poppy did not return to Daphne's home right away. Lavinia and her stepmother had urged her to return under the baron's roof, claiming it was more proper. Evidently, they worried others in society might gossip about Poppy being a guest at Daphne when her sister was so comfortably situated.

Poppy spent the day indoors with her sisters, catching up on the last several days. Surprisingly with none of the usual snark from her stepmother and sisters. Possibly due to the presence of the amiable baron. They had an early supper, and then Poppy spent the rest of the evening in the library reading. Intending to retire early, Poppy hurried up the stairs and down the hallway. She paused at the sound of loud voices. They came from the small library on the second floor.

"Compromise the earl? Mama, please. I cannot do what you ask!"

"Rubbish! Lord Kingsley is determined to make a fool of himself over your sister. We must be prudent and plan several steps ahead. You saw how he has been, dancing only with her for the entire season."

Poppy's stomach lurched sickeningly, and she pressed a hand over her mouth.

"Mama, please, I do not wish to—"

"Do you wish to be a countess?"

Silence fell, and she imagined Rebecca fidgeting.

"You will do as I say. Lavinia and I have it well planned. Your sister will ensure a few society matrons arrive at the library at the opportune time at tonight's ball. You will ensure when the door opens that you are in the earl's arms. Trip yourself or faint, but ensure you are in his arms and prevaricate to stay there until the door opens."

There were several rustles, and their voices faded until Poppy could no longer discern their scheme. What a designing creature her sister and stepmother proved to be! It was quite fine for them to order Rebecca to encourage the earl, but to deceitfully entrap him into marriage was a selfish and despicable act. There was a peculiar and very heavy chill upon Poppy's heart that Rebecca might succeed.

Poppy hurried down the hallway and into her room. She leaned against the door and listened until she heard Rebecca enter her own room. Taking a deep breath, Poppy left her room and made her way to her sister's room. She knocked once and was bid enter. It shocked her to see the red puffiness of Rebecca's eyes.

"You were crying," Poppy said gently.

"What do you want?" her sister demanded, dropping a piece of lace she had been caressing. "Are you here to gloat about the earl once again dancing only with you?"

With another startling jolt, Poppy realized that might have been the only reason her stepmother decided to take matters into her hands.

"The earl is not attracted to me, Rebecca," Poppy said, pushing the words past the aching tightness in her throat.

"That is because you do not see how he looks at you." This was said bitterly. "He does not regard me at all, and if he does, it is to speak to me in a manner as if I am a younger sister."

Poppy took a steadying breath. "I overheard what mother said to you just now. She wants you to compromise Lord Kingsley and start a scandal." She hurried over to her sister. "You must not, Rebecca! To act in such a manner will surely destroy your reputation and create discord between you and the earl. He is not the sort of man to be forced against his heart and wishes. I do not believe he will offer you marriage even if you are caught in a compromising position!"

Rebecca's face crumpled, and fresh tears sprang to her eyes. "Mama and Lavinia say I must if I wish to secure a happy future. But I do not love the earl; I truly do not."

Poppy paused, assessing the pained lovelorn look on her sister's face. "Is there someone…someone that you like?"

They had never confided in each other before, and it had always been Rebecca and Lavinia that had the close relationship, with Poppy looking inward and dearly hoping to be a part of their happiness. Rebecca flung herself into Poppy's arms, startling her. There she allowed her sister to cry out her frustration while she patted her shoulders and muttered soothing nonsense.

Finally, when the storm had passed, Rebecca stepped away.

"You must think me a silly watering pot."

"No," Poppy said softly. "You are a young girl in her first season, and you face immense pressure to make a good match and not disappoint mother. It did not occur to me how hard this must be for you."

A tremulous smile crossed Rebecca's lips. "There… there is a gentleman I quite fancy." She blushed and looked away for a few moments. "Mr. Langston is only two and twenty. He is very well liked and comes from a good family. He…he likes me as well, I can tell!"

"Have you told mother?"

"Mama says I am not to dance with him anymore, and the drive out that I agreed to must be canceled."

"Is Mr. Langston not from a respectable family?"

"He is not an earl," she whispered miserably, tears pooling in her eyes. "How can I not agree with mama and Lavinia?"

"Does that matter very much to you?" Poppy gently asked. She had always assumed Rebecca to be greatly persuaded by Lavinia. It cheered her to know that Rebecca's feelings and emotions were not wholly manipulated to suit her sister and stepmother's lofty aspirations.

"He is not bumbling or poor. He has an inheritance of five thousand pounds a year. Mr. Langston treats me with great cordiality and affection. He also scolds me when I am puffed up with vanity and say nonsensical things. No…no other gentleman has ever taken me to task. They are all too busy appreciating my beauty or trying to impress me."

"I daresay it can be tiresome if no one looks beneath the surface of your beauty."

"Oh, but Mr. Langston does! He is most amiable and charming, and when we speak, he asks my opinion on all matters and subjects. And he truly listens to what I have to say. He is most considerate. Wyatt…sorry…Mr. Langston makes me laugh."

"Then be honest with mother and let her know you hold him in your regards."

"I cannot," she wailed. "How can I go against what mama says? How do I dare?"

"Rebecca—"

The door crashed open, and Lavinia framed the doorway, a light rose-colored gown draped over her arm. She affected a dramatic pause when she saw Poppy.

"Why was I not invited to this tête-à-tête?" she asked with a light laugh. However, her eyes were curious and deeply assessing. "Is everything well, Rebecca?"

Their younger sister hurriedly wiped away the remnants of her tears. "Why, yes, of course. I am but nervous and excited for tonight's ball."

Concern rushed through Poppy, and she turned to Lavinia. "What you are asking Rebecca to do is beyond the pale and—"

"No!" Rebecca cried, hurrying to Poppy's side, grasping her hand, and squeezing. "I am quite fine. Thank you, Poppy, for checking in on me. I would like to be alone now."

"Rebecca—"

"Please leave!"

Poppy responded to the desperate plea in her sister's eyes and voice and excused herself. Once outside, she leaned against the door and heard Rebecca explain she had a migraine, and Poppy helped. She understood her sister's position. Rebecca was afraid to go against their mother and Lavinia and earn their displeasure. How could she when Rebecca had no power or position of her own?

Poppy went to her room only a few doors down, walked over to the fireplace and held out her hands to warm them. The day had been unexpectedly chilly, and a similar coldness wormed inside her heart. Her stepmother's scheme was beyond improper and outlandish. It was also cruel.

"And why should I care?" Poppy whispered, pacing.

The memory of the hot, urgent kisses James had pressed to her mouth bloomed in her memory and sent heat curling low in her belly. "Oh! I must stop thinking of him in this manner. We are friends, nothing more." *Friends who sometimes kissed each other so wonderfully and passionately.*

Swallowing down the groan, she hurried to the armoire and picked out a coat and a hat. She searched until she found a veil. Poppy waited until her sisters and mother had already set out to the ball. There was not a moment to waste. The earl was normally late in arriving at any ball he showed up at. Poppy could only hope tonight would be the same.

Hurrying down the winding staircase, she went out the kitchen and the back entrance. She would head to James's house and warn him of the terrible plot afoot. If he was not there, then he would be left to his own devices to escape her sister and stepmother's machinations.

CHAPTER 13

I cannot afford such sentiments, nor do I hunger for them.

What a load of crock, and he had been the one to say them. He had to. In Poppy's eyes, he had seen the very sentiments that stirred violently in his heart. James was failing to stay away from Poppy. He was failing in falling for her. He was bloody *failing*. James's duty was clear and simple. Save his family's estate and restore it to its former glory. That would take hard work and several more years, but he would leave an inheritance to his sons and daughters he would be rightfully proud of.

Secondly, he must honor Henry's oath. That would see James married and fulfilling another duty of getting his heir. He could feel the flames eating away at his well-laid plans. Poppy had ruffled the calm waters of his existence, casting him into a state of unwelcomed restlessness and constant longing.

Worse, James did not understand fully what he felt for her.

I cannot afford such sentiments, nor do I hunger for them.

He pushed from behind his desk, walked over to the sideboard and poured brandy into a glass. James then downed the contents in one long, burning swallow. "What if I have fallen in love?" he muttered, thinking on her softly spoken words the last time he held her in his arms.

I am going to miss you, Poppy; I already do.

Pressing his palm against the cool windowpane, James hung his head. "Damn it all to hell, am I not already there?"

James constantly wished to lift the burdens from her shoulders and see Poppy smile. *Was that love?*

Her lively sense of humor and quick wit were rather endearing. He hungered to kiss her always and even shamelessly to do more. His dreams of her could be explicitly carnal in nature, and even when he berated himself in the mornings, the very next night, the same dream would recur. Poppy splayed naked before him on silken sheets, her curves on wanton display and those beautiful eyes dark with need. And he would touch and kiss her all over until she was wild and sobbing for him.

There were times when around her, James felt like the basest of creatures. She was all softness. Every delectable inch of her. And her mouth…the taste of her should be outlawed and banished. The woman was pure temptation. It had taken every ounce of restraint he possessed to not succumb to the artless temptation in her gaze and kiss and ravish her without thoughts of consequences.

Other times he simply wanted to sit with her and listen to the softness of her voice, the laughter lurking there while she told him an anecdote. Or he just wanted to ride with her or sit and have a conversation. Should he cast his worries on her, James knew she would listen and offer insight. Her kindness was dependable.

Scrubbing a hand over his face, James glanced at the pile of paperwork on his desk. He had been working since morning, tallying the returns from several investments. Over twenty-five thousand pounds had come to him at the end of the month, and with a few strokes of his pen, it had all gone into the estate, to creditors, and some toward Poppy's dowry.

A quick glance at his watch showed it was barely ten p.m. He had promised Daphne to attend some ball tonight, but James was not in the mood. Yet a promise was a promise. And for the first time, he wished Henry had found another means to save their estate.

James did not want to marry Miss Winters when she came of age. Even if she came with another one hundred thousand pounds and already promised to be an uncommon beauty. Whom he wanted was Miss Poppy Ashford, and he could not have her.

Swallowing down another drink, James set the glass down with a *clink*. He would ring his valet and make himself presentable for the ball. He was certain Poppy would be there, and he would do his damnedest to stay away from her. Or dance with her one last time.

No, bloody hell no. That was what he had said two nights ago, and he had taken that final dance. James had done his duty there. He had seen the bucks staring at her the last time he danced with her, practically salivating and tripping over themselves to ask her to the dancefloor. It always astonished him how damn stupid his own sex could be, as if he would ever need someone else to show him that

Poppy was a rare and beautiful treasure only because someone else paid her attention.

Hurrying from his study and down the long hallway, James skidded to a halt in the doorway at the veiled lady his butler had only just allowed entry.

"Who should I inform His Lordship has called?" his butler asked, glaring at her veil.

There was no doubt she had badgered the man to gain admittance. James would recognize that slight sensual shape anywhere, and the way she walked—confident and as if she were always in a hurry, proclaimed his mysterious visitor to be Miss Poppy Ashford. A quick glance did not reveal that she was hurt or suffering from any injuries. Relief sliced through him, and then the reality of the situation truly sank in his bones.

Bloody hell. She was here. Under his roof. Alone with him. A loud roar filled James's head, and his loins grew heavy on a painful rush of desire.

This was disastrous. James did the only thing he could in the situation.

"You will turn around and return home at once!" he ordered in a tone that would suffer no rebuttal, only instant obedience.

Then he turned and ran.

<hr />

Poppy stared in astonishment as James ran in loping bounds up the staircase of his home. The butler made a choked sound as she hurried after him. "James, what are you doing? I must meet with you right away!"

"Milady," the butler cried, rushing after her.

James paused, gripping the banister. "Did I not tell you to leave?"

"Yes, but that I am here and in disguise should tell you it is clearly a matter of grave importance."

A pained grimace crossed his face. "I will find you later and speak of it."

"It might very well be too late then! I overheard a matter of importance that is related to you." She lowered her voice and glanced back at the butler on her heels when she said this, not wanting servants to get a hint of anything that might involve Rebecca. Poppy knew firsthand that servants loved to gossip, and most scandals from private homes were spread by them.

"I will bear it in mind," he said. "I shall call on you tomorrow."

Then he continued up the stairs. Poppy gaped at his retreating back. What in the world was he about? Why was he acting in this strange and odious manner? Tomorrow would be too late. He would attend the ball tonight, and then he would be trapped in her stepmother's scheme.

Poppy sprinted up the stairs with a muttered curse, leaving the butler in a confused daze at its base. Upon reaching the landing, she was just in time to see James closing a door down the hallway. What in heavens was happening? Hurrying to that door, she tested the doorknob and found it locked.

Poppy knocked on the door. "James?"

No answer came forth. She knocked again, and still, the dratted man refused to come to the door. Poppy would leave a note for him and damn his silly hide. He would owe her an explanation for this behavior. She walked away, and her steps faltered. He would occupy the master chamber, so the room beside his should be an adjoining one. Poppy tested that knob, and it opened noiselessly under her palm. She hurried to the connecting door, opened it and spilled into James' room.

He was there, pacing like a caged lion and raking his fingers through his hair. At Poppy's entrance, he whirled toward her, his lips parting in shock.

"James, I must tell you. I overheard my…my stepmother plotting to compromise you most thoroughly at tonight's ball. You must not attend it. That is what I wanted to share with you, but you ran away from me. What is wrong with you?"

"I told you to leave," he growled.

"Well, yes…you did…James. Why are you removing your jacket?"

Next, his shoes came off, and with an almost violent motion, he tugged his shirttails from his pants.

"I tried to stay away from you. I really did. But then you are here, in my chambers, where all the carnal fantasies I've had of you happened. I've fisted my cock to the very image of you, and you are here."

Oh, dear. "Do you mean to ravish me?" Poppy demanded a bit breathlessly, wondering why she was not running.

"Every delectable inch of you."

That promise had heat blossoming through her body, and her sex ached unexpectedly.

"So my dearest, Poppy, run. I'll not chase you, but I do

not have the willpower to deny myself you anymore. Every night I dream of you…and you are here."

Her heart jerked so fast Poppy felt dizzy. "Every night, I think of you as well, James. You…You are more than a friend. You are someone I crave." The confession felt torn from her very soul.

James made a strange sound when she removed her hat and veil, tossed it onto the chaise longue, and toed off her shoes.

"You are not running."

"Only unless it is into your arms," she said softly, her heart beating so fast she felt faint. "I want this…I want *you*."

He held out his arms, and she hurtled herself forward. James gathered her into his arms, dragging her up against his body, pulling her mouth up to meet his, invading with his tongue. His kiss was passionate and so very wonderful. With a muffled moan, she moved her mouth under his, kissing him back with every emotion burning inside for him.

He dragged his mouth from hers and pressed it to her ears. "This is damnably reckless."

"I know." And she did, for no marriage would come from him. At least not for three years. Yet Poppy could not bear for this moment to ever end. She was painfully aroused and gripped by emotions she had never felt before. "I do not want to be rational or good or biddable. Tonight, I want you, James, in all the ways I have been dreaming."

With a muttered curse, he took her mouth over and over, in sweet and other times hard, desperate kisses. Poppy dazedly realized he had unbuttoned her jacket and full skirts. Her dress, chemise, laces, and corset were removed with kisses in between. She should have been a nervous mess, but that book had prepared her.

Soon James was naked, and so was Poppy. Before shyness could overcome her, he swung her into his arms, and within a few strides, they were by his bed, tumbling down on the soft mattress. They kissed endlessly until her body grew fevered, until the ache between her legs was pulsing wetness. Until she was twisting and tugging at his shoulders, demanding something she was not familiar with. Poppy felt as if she would disintegrate under the lash of heated arousal pulsing throughout her body.

But James seemed as if he could not stop kissing her. Her mouth, her cheeks, the curves of her throat, down to her breasts. He sucked a nipple into his mouth, and Poppy slapped a hand over her mouth, a low moan breaking from her.

She had never imagined such sensations were possible.

"James, I need…I…ahh," she cried out when he nibbled at her sensitive nipple then laved it with his tormenting tongue.

One of James's hands drifted over her body, molding and shaping, teasing, and tormenting. His fingers brushed over the hollow of her throat, over the aching mounds of her breasts and seared a path over her quivering stomach down to her thighs. His fingers found her damp curls, gliding through slick folds, sinking deep into her tight, wet sex. And the entire time, he kissed her mouth with breathtaking intensity.

All of Poppy's senses were assaulted with piercing desire. Her flesh felt sensitized and needy. She nudged her hips, and his finger moved within her. It was as if lightning struck her low in her belly and traveled down to her sex.

Poppy pulled her mouth from James's, breathing raggedly at the strange but wonderful feeling. She gasped as his thumb glided over her nub of pleasure. The friction had her arching her hips more into his wicked caress. James licked down her body, following the path his fingers had taken earlier, kissing and nipping all over her body, paying attention to the quivering softness of her belly. Then he went even lower. A kiss from his scorching lips skimmed her inner thigh. Poppy trembled—the ache spreading to her belly.

His fingers moved from her body, and she cried out her protest. Now she felt empty when she desperately needed to be filled. James cupped her buttocks in both his palms, tilting her hips, dipped his head, kissing her deeply in the sensitive place between her legs. That deep, heated lick across her folds ripped a wild cry from Poppy. The pleasure was sharp and searing, flowering from her nub and throughout her entire body. Poppy sobbed, and quaked, and lifted her hips to his mouth for more. He licked her over and over, dragging his tongue over her pearl of pleasure, before sucking her wetly into his mouth. Sweet, bone-shattering ecstasy tore through Poppy, and she cried out, gripping the sheets at her side.

He rose above her, settling his weight between her open thighs. James lowered his head and kissed her, and to her mortified shock, the carnal taste of herself on his tongue aroused her senses even more. He reached between them, and then there was a hard pressure at her entrance. Without relinquishing her mouth, he pressed forward. A tight pressure seemed to invade her, and she whimpered. James paused, then plunged forward, burying his length deep inside her. Pain buffeted her senses, and he placed soft, soothing kisses along the tip of her nose and her mouth.

"The pain will soon pass, I promise it," he said gruffly.

The clenching emptiness and the aloneness she had endured for so long were filled. A long sigh of pleasure escaped her, and she wrapped her hands around his neck. "I trust you, James."

He jolted in her arms, then, with a harsh groan, buried his face in the curve of her neck. James withdrew from her and thrust deep. Poppy cried out at the overwhelming sensation of his manhood filling her once more. He lifted his face from her neck, held her gaze, refusing to release her, and began to ride her in a deep, hard, beautiful rhythm.

Pleasure mingled with pain with each deep erotic plunge and retreat. Poppy wrapped her legs high around his hips. Her arousal deepened despite lifting her legs, for it clasped him even deeper inside her body, making the aching pressure in her sex more overwhelming.

It was ecstasy. She writhed beneath him, hips arching, craving to get closer. The coil in her belly drew tighter and tighter, and the pleasure burned hotter. Distantly she became aware of her thighs trembling, of her wetness, of the almost painful need closing around her entire body. That coil burst, and Poppy could only gasp as the most nerve-wracking pleasure she had ever felt tore through her body, leaving her drained and sated.

James kissed her, and seconds later, he hugged her into a tight embrace, and with a groan, found his own release.

"Bloody hell," she said against his mouth. "That was beautiful."

James laughed, his shoulders shaking. "You perfectly echoed my sentiments."

He gently withdrew from her and gathered her into the curve of his arms.

"Why would you run from this?" she asked after a breathless moment.

He stiffened. "Poppy—"

"I know," she said gently and with soft humor.

"I can only offer you now...this moment. It is the reason I tried to stay away from you because I know I am not able to make you promises. Promises you so richly deserve."

She shifted in his arms, turning onto his chest so she could see his face. Poppy touched his mouth with trembling fingers. "I am not a debutante that was ruthlessly seduced by a bounder. I *allowed* you to ravage me because I wanted you...I wanted *this*. No other reason."

They stared at each other for long moments before he slowly nodded. "I am going to clean us up, and then...."

"Yes?"

"We are going to do this all over again."

Poppy's laugh was swallowed by his tender kiss against her bruised and well-ravished mouth. Oh yes, she most definitely wanted to do this again.

CHAPTER 14

I'll be sure to marry you, Poppy Ashford. Somehow I'll find a way.

Had Poppy heard those words when she drifted off into exhausted slumber snuggled inside James's arms? When he had roused her from her sleep only an hour later, it had been to get her to dress hurriedly, and then they bundled into his carriage to take her home. He had even alighted from the equipage some houses down from her sister's townhome, ensured her veil was fixed and assured her he would call on her soon. It wasn't until Poppy had sneaked inside the home through the kitchens and run to her room that she recalled that faint promise at her temple.

Poppy was not sure what to call what they had done three times last night. She had been thoroughly ravished. It had been perfectly wonderful *and* breathlessly pleasurable. Her cheeks heated, and Poppy did her best to direct her thoughts to memories that did not cause her heart to stutter and her entire body to flush.

She had to come up with a plan once again. She could

not marry another when she was in love with James. He might never marry her or anyone else until three years had passed. Poppy needed to understand the fullness of that oath. And she was almost certain she could not remain living with her stepmother and stepsisters anymore. It also felt wrong to take any money from James, knowing how hard he worked and that his estates were still in the red.

Poppy was not afraid of working as a governess. A rueful smile curved her mouth that she had come full circle.

A sharp knock sounded, and she lifted her fingers from the piano keys. Her gentle playing over the last thirty minutes was perhaps irritating her stepmother as it always did, and the butler was here to inform her of it.

"Yes?"

The butler opened the door. "A Mr. Winters has called for you, Miss Poppy. He awaits you in the small parlor."

"Mr. Winters?"

"Yes."

Was he perhaps another suitor? "Is my stepmother here?"

"No, Miss Poppy, Mrs. Ashford has gone out with Lady Hayes and Miss Rebecca."

Poppy stood, smoothed down the lines of her day gown, and made her way to the parlor. A gentleman did indeed wait for her, seated in an armchair with a cup of tea in his hands. Except she was not at all familiar with him. This Mr. Winters was quite handsome with his wavy black hair and athletic build. The man was immaculately dressed in dark trousers and jacket, with a burgundy waistcoat and at this first glance, it was clear he was an affluent man of some distinction.

"Miss Ashford," he said, standing when she entered.

Poppy dipped into a slight curtsy. "Mr. Winters, you have me at a disadvantage. I do not know who you are, but you seem to know me…even where to call upon me."

"How forthright you are," he murmured caustically.

His tone surprised her, and she frowned. Thankfully, she had left the door slightly ajar. The butler and a few footmen were within shouting distance. Poppy was also not afraid to slap him over the head with one of the vases should it become necessary.

"Who are you, sir, and why did you wish to meet with me?"

An icy smile touched his mouth, and dark green eyes rudely scanned her body. "I am curious to know why you are mentioned so much in the company of my daughter's intended. It is odd, you see, for he has kept to himself these past few years, but now every scandal sheet feels it worthwhile to mention Lord Kingsley and Miss Ashford together in the same breath. Why?"

Shock blossomed through her in a chilly wave. It took her a moment to catch her breath, but when she finally did, it was to ask, "Lord Kingsley is to be *married* to your daughter?"

He reached into his pocket and withdrew a rolled paper tied with a ribbon. "Yes. I assume you know he is to marry in three years. We have a betrothal agreement, and I will sue him for breach of promise should he try to cry off."

Poppy reeled, and a sickening sensation entered her stomach. She did not trust herself to make a civil reply. With an effort of will, she maintained a serene expression. "Have you finished your piece, Mr. Winters?" Poppy politely asked.

Sharp and cunning eyes assessed every nuance of her features. Undoubtedly the man searched for any evidence that there was a serious attachment between her and the earl.

"I suggest you understand my meaning of this meeting, Miss Ashford?"

"Of course I do. You rudely barged into my sister's home without observing the correct proprieties in calling at one's home after noon merely to ascertain if there is an attachment between Lord Kingsley and myself. You then decided to be as ruthless as possible and to use your wealth and words to cut such a thread had it existed. I assure you, Lord Kingsley is merely kind in helping a spinster get the proper notice to land her a decent offer. There is no sort of attachment between us. Your visit was boorish and unnecessary."

Winters's eyes had hardened at her speech, and as he stood, he tugged at his neckcloth as if made uncomfortable.

"I will pay you twenty thousand pounds to immediately cease all connections with the earl. Whether they be false or not."

Poppy stepped back, her hand fluttering to her chest. "I beg your pardon?"

"Twenty thousand pounds will be my only offer. Do not play coy for more."

"You heard me. It is not real," she said, clenching her fist tightly against the pain piercing her belly.

"I know what I saw," Mr. Winters hissed unexpectedly. "I watched as he walked with you along Rotten Row last week, and then when he danced with you at Lady Bloomfield's ball. That blasted earl had the look of a man *desperately* in love. You might think it is not real, Miss Ashbrook, but I am a man. I know hunger when I see it."

The breath whooshed from her, and Poppy's cheeks heated. James stared at her with undisguised hunger, and this man knew it? "You do not know James," she said quietly.

That hawk-like gaze sharpened, and his lips curled. "James, is it?"

"Yes, James…Lord Kingsley…is my friend." Poppy lifted her chin. "He has *honor*. If he made you a promise to marry your daughter, he would honor that promise, even at the cost of his own happiness." She glanced at the contract he had waved before her. "He will not break or dishonor that promise. Ever. It is against his character as a gentleman to do so. If you are overly concerned about the earl keeping his promise, I urge you to pay him a visit and discuss it in a gentleman-like manner."

Mr. Winters stared at her for a long time, and Poppy did not wilt under his hard scrutiny but lifted her chin and held his regard. A glint of admiration entered his hardened eyes.

"I understand the appeal," he finally murmured before bowing, donning his hat and walking away.

Poppy dropped without any form of grace onto the

sofa and buried her face in her hands. "Oh, James." It shocked her to feel the wetness on her face.

They had never stood a chance. All the dreams blooming in her heart, the bubbling love, and the hope that if she waited until he was ready to marry, he might choose her vanished like ashes in the wind. It hurt. Deeply. For she had fallen in love with him, and despite knowing better, had dreamed such dreams of being his lover…his wife…his countess.

Silly, I am beyond silly.

❦

JAMES HAD WOKEN this morning with the knowledge he could not marry Miss Vinnette Winters, and he would have to break the oath his brother made. It had gutted him, but the thought of breaking Poppy's heart destroyed him. If he had to choose between his honor…between Henry's honor and Poppy, his choice was clear.

It had shocked him that he could be so certain that he loved her beyond honor and consequences. With her by his side, he could face any hurdle, and even if it took years, they would overcome it. He had risen early, engaged in a bout of vigorous boxing with Worsley while James plotted what he could offer Mr. Winters for the dishonor of breaking the oath.

If the man wanted to duel, though it was highly illegal, James would oblige. His thoughts had raced in several directions, and he had decided the only way forward was to visit Winters. Now James sat in the man's study, awaiting his presence for almost an hour before Mr. Winters entered.

James kept his expression inscrutable as he stared at Mr. Winters.

"You wish to break the agreement," the man murmured in a dangerous undertone. "I believe that is what I am hearing."

"Yes," James said flatly. "My brother, Henry, was desperate when he made this bargain, and I am thankful you were there to help him. It helped us restore several of our estates and kept me on the path I am on now in recovering my inheritance. I cannot honor Henry's oath to make your daughter the Countess of Kingsley. I have my reasons for it. Upon my honor, I vow that the connection you sought from my family can be maintained without a marriage alliance. While I am not able to marry Miss Winters, the full connections and circumstance of my family will be made available to her when she is ready to come out in society." James stood, holding the glass of brandy in a tight clasp. "I will also repay the sum you gave my brother. I only asked we draft up an agreement and a reasonable timeframe for me to repay it. I ask for five years."

A very tight and almost impossible timeframe, but he would work his fingers to the bones if necessary.

Mr. Winters considered him with his cold, piercing green eyes. "I assume this change of heart is because of Miss Poppy Ashford. I understand. Our meeting was brief, but she is a remarkable woman. Fierce. Loyal. Qualities I admire."

James stiffened, an icy feeling moving through his heart. "You approached Miss Ashford?"

"Yes, I was most interested in knowing why she spent so much time with my daughter's intended."

A cold fury blew through James. "You dared?"

Mr. Winters stood, leaned forward, and slammed his hands down on his desk. "When I saw your name mentioned in the scandal sheets with this unknown lady, it surprised me. Since you became aware of the agreement, you have courted no lady, not even taken a mistress to your bed!"

"So you took it upon yourself to spy on me?" James demanded, outraged by the man's gall. "Who do you think you are…and who do you think I am? You dared to follow and spy on my personal business?"

"I dared, more than once, and I saw how you looked at Miss Ashford!"

"How I look at her is not your goddamn business," James snapped. "It is not the conduct of a gentleman to approach a lady to speak with her of business she has no knowledge of."

"And is it the conduct of a gentleman to break his oaths?"

"Yes," James said quietly. "Especially if the bonds of that oath will see me hurting your daughter who is an innocent. And if it will see me hurting the woman I have fallen in love with."

At the mention of causing his daughter pain, Winters stiffened.

"I love Miss Ashford, and there is nothing under this sun that can change that. Should I continue on this path and marry your daughter, I would give her my respect and fidelity but not much else. She is deserving of better. You want her to be a countess, to have connections within society. I can help her. My family can help her when she is ready. That I can swear to and fulfill."

Winters fisted his hands at his side. "I will sue you."

James stared at him, a hollow pit opening inside. He had known the risk of this when he ventured here, and he was willing to assume it. "If you must. I will meet you in court and let them be the judge of our situation. I was not bound to complete the promise Henry made. I did so because I still had your money. I am now offering to repay that money…with interest and still be a connection for your daughter when she is ready. That is a fair and honorable bargain."

"How brave and unflinching you are," Winters sneered.

"I must be when it comes to Miss Ashford."

Winters chuckled mirthlessly. "To be young and in love. You see, I promised Vinette's mother I would see her rise in society and become a toast of the haute monde. I will not break that promise, and by God neither will you."

"I *must*," James rasped hoarsely, pain slicing him deep. "Allow me to use my influence to benefit your family. Allow me to return the money you gave my brother."

"I know of your circumstances! You do not have the money to repay me! And I will not release you from this agreement. I will sue and cause a great scandal. I promise it will follow you like a great stench for years!"

"No, you will not," James said with ruthless precision,

walking over. "Do you think me a fool? Do you believe you are the only one capable of cunning and calculation?"

Winters's face smoothed into a mask.

James stared at him. "You will do nothing to ruin your daughter's chances. Whatever scandal you throw on me… you will have thrown on yourself and also on her. No one knows of our betrothal…or of this business arrangement you made with my brother. I suspect you kept it that way as a contingency should it fail; your daughter's reputation would not be affected, and no one could say she was jilted. I have not even told my mother about this arrangement…I did not even reveal it to Poppy, whom I love and trust."

James waved a hand. "You are trying to bend me to your will, but I am my own man. Allow me to cancel this contract Henry made and take me up on my offer to support your daughter's come-out with the full force and connections of my name and title."

A heavy silence lingered in the man's study.

Then he said, "I will give you thirty days to repay the money. Not a day more."

James jolted. "Thirty days is impossible."

"Those are my terms. Should you fail to meet them, I will sue for breach of promise and damn all our reputations to hell. My daughter loves Paris. She will happily stay there for the rest of her life, and that way, the disgrace will only stick to you and Miss Ashford. Repay me in thirty days or marry my daughter."

James stared at his resolution and then turned and walked away. Once outside, he lifted his face to the sun. What a damn mess. He had to see Poppy right away. James had to explain to her. He hurried to call his carriage and supplied his coachman with her address. They rumbled away, and James saw no way in which he could drum up that money in a year, much less a month.

A flash of blue and a swaying hip caught his eyes. It was Poppy. James rapped on the roof of his carriage and bounded from the equipage without waiting for the steps.

"Poppy!"

She whirled around, and he faltered. Her eyes were red and pained. She had been crying.

James hurried to her side, careful to keep a respectable distance as they were in public.

"James," she said with a small smile.

"I am coming from Mr. Winters's home. He told me of his visit to you. I am sorry for it. He should not have presumed to speak to you." James raked a hand through his hair, absently realizing he had left his hat in the carriage. "Poppy, I should have told you."

"You made me no false promises," she said softly. "Whatever wound there is to my heart is because of my own foolish hopes. I cannot blame you for it. You have been a great friend and supporter. I wish you all the best."

Then she whirled around. Uncaring they might have an audience, he grabbed her elbow. When she paused, he moved to stand in front of her.

"I am not marrying her, Poppy; I cannot, not when I love you."

Her eyes widened. "*What?*"

"I love you."

Tears spilled down her cheeks, and she hurriedly wiped them away. "I love you too, but you…you promised to marry her. Surely you cannot break that. She will be devastated. Her chances and reputation will be ruined. I...*no*, James!"

"It is not what you are thinking. She is fourteen, and I suspect she might not even know about this arrangement. My brother made the promise to marry her when she is of age," he said gruffly. "I was simply trying to fulfill it because he died before he could."

"And Mr. Winters agrees to this?"

"No. He wants me to repay a sum of one hundred thousand pounds in a month, or he will sue."

She flinched and lifted wounded eyes to his. "Even I know such a scandal would be catastrophic for you, Daphne, and your mother. Your entire family will be affected."

James looked away, the truth of her words resounding deeply inside. "Poppy—"

"No," she said softly. "I love you, James. Too much to want that for you. I love Daphne. She is young and has ample time to remarry and have a wonderful life. That will be very hard to achieve with a ruined reputation and her brother's honor sunken beyond reproach."

It was James's turn to flinch.

"We shall remain great friends, and I shall never forget you." Then to his shock, she leaned forward, pressed a kiss to his cheek, turned around and continued walking.

THAT NIGHT, James sat in Worsley's gambling den, nursing his third glass of whisky. He stood apart from the general excitement which pulsed in the air. The Club's decor was one of luxury; red and green carpets covered the floor, and swaths of red and golden garlands twined themselves around massive white Corinthian columns. Worsley's club was popular, and it was a busy and energetic night. Every table on the floor—faro, hazard, whist, and even the roulette wheels was filled with ladies and gentlemen hoping to take home winnings from one of the tables.

James felt as if he had lost everything—the honor he thought he was protecting for so many years and the lady he had fallen irrevocably in love with.

"The simplest solution would be to marry Miss Winters," Worsley said. "Winters is known to me. He is ruthless when crossed. Your brother did not enter this deal with an easy man."

Everything inside of James recoiled at the notion. The remembered pain and hope in Poppy's eyes haunted him. She loved him enough to fight for his honor while he loved her enough to dismiss it. What a blasted mess. "No, I'll not marry Miss Winters."

Smoke wafted through the air from the many lit cigars, glasses clinked loudly, and the clattering of dice echoed as they rolled on the tables as if mocking the calm assurance James wanted to present to the world. Inside he was a mess of pain and desperation. He could not lose Poppy.

"You have already lost Miss Ashford," Worsley said. "It seems she genuinely loves you. She wants to protect you from the consequences of this damnable agreement Henry made. Whyever did you not tell me about it?"

"What is done is done," James said, leaning back in the chair and knocking back his drink. "Daphne told me earlier Poppy is leaving town. She has no money. She has no connections. And it is unbearable for her to live with her mother and sisters anymore. She is brave enough to try and find a living on her own."

"You are worried for her."

"I am petrified at the thought of her alone, without any funds or support. I combed through my books earlier, trying to find where to take the money to write a bank draft. There is nothing. I will have to wait weeks for a few of the investments to cash in. I have thought about selling a few of our paintings and even silverware. I cannot allow her to disappear without any money."

Worsley considered him.

"I will not take your money, so don't bother offering." It was a desperate situation, but he could not presume upon his friend's kindness in such a great manner. The sum was a small fortune after all.

"Have you ever thought about the fighting pits?"

James frowned. "Your underground fighting pits?"

"Yes."

He glanced upward where some patrons climbed the staircase to the second floor and strolled with excitement in their steps toward the fighting club. There they placed even greater wagers on men who participated in the brutal sport of bare-knuckle brawling while disguised patrons watched, smoking cigars and drinking brandy.

"Surely you jest."

"Many lords of society take part in my matches. Surely you are familiar with the Earl of Maschelly. He won most of his fortune in the fighting pits. And he is not the only one."

It seemed farfetched, but it was entirely possible. James

was only seven and twenty and had spent the last few years working to restore his inheritance to surpass its former glory. Worsley's gambling den was still considered one of the golden halls and in the caliber of Brooks, White's, and The Cocoa Tree. However, it had also garnered a reputation of wicked profligacy like many clubs in Soho Square because of the fighting den. Many lords might have participated here in the highly illegal bare-knuckle fighting for money. "I have heard of him. I recall a rumor from a couple years or so ago that he took a lady there to the rings."

"Yes, she is now his countess."

"She fought someone?"

"She kicked a libertine in the balls."

James chuckled. While he had heard about the couple, he had not personally met them. James looked again to the staircase. "What kind of fortunes are made there?"

"The purse tonight is fifteen thousand pounds."

James choked on the next sip of his brandy. "What?"

"You heard me. I can slip you in to fight instead of Viscount Markham."

James's heart was pounding fiercely. If he could win this money for Poppy. "I have no experience."

"Every gentleman can box. You were a soldier, and I know you were not an idle one. What have you to lose? The money is also paid out immediately. I want you to know the laws which govern pugilism are not observed here. It is primal fighting…raw and gritty. Win by whatever it takes."

And it was with that, James found himself an hour later in the ring stripped to the waist, thin leather strips that had been soaked in water or perhaps vinegar wrapped around his fists. He had practiced boxing from when he was a lad; but, as Worsley had cautioned, this would be pure, brutal, barbaric fighting. For money. *Bloody hell.* He was really doing this. Glancing around the dimmed room, James noted the tables were less raucous, and only a handful of ladies or perhaps members of the demi-monde sat amongst the lords and gentlemen there. Smoke curled around the room, and footmen darted adroitly between the tables delivering drinks to the patrons betting on the fight's outcome.

James was not familiar with the man entering the ring, and the hush from the audience became almost respectful. The man's body was muscled, more so than James's, and the look in the man's eyes was almost feral.

The match started, and they danced around each other for several minutes before the man threw a punch. James's head snapped back, and before he could recover, several powerful blows landed against his torso and on his chin. He fell to the ground with a resounding thud. The pain was alive inside his body. He vaguely heard a man counting, giving him time to stand.

James struggled to his feet, inhaling deeply and breathing through the pain. He was not an idle hand. He was skilled in boxing, fencing, and pistols. This was just another burden to bear on his shoulders for the sake of those he loved, for he had already decided this was how he would repay Mr. Winters his money. One fight at a time. Even if it left him bloody and broken.

James sank into a place deep inside, buried the pain, lifted his fists and waded in, to fight.

CHAPTER 15

"Poppy!"

She paused in climbing the steps of the carriage at her name and turned around. James was walking toward her, and the determination that had formed in her heart trembled. Poppy cast a glance at Daphne, who had come to see her off.

"You told him I was leaving today?"

Her friend smiled apologetically. "Yes. I know it is painful for you to see him. However, James suspected I was loaning you my carriage and a footman and maid for your journey and coaxed the knowledge from me."

Poppy swallowed, then jolted in shock when he came to a stop some feet away. His face was a mess of purple and black bruises. One of his eyelids was swollen closed, and his knuckles were rubbed raw. Yet there was a smile about his mouth.

"James," she said faintly, tears springing to her eyes. "What happened? Did Mr. Winters attack you?"

"No, I assure you I am fine."

Her anxious mind, relieved of its worst fears, she asked, "Why are you here?"

She noted his set face, his clamped mouth, and stiffly held arms. He was in pain.

His mouth curved, but it was a bleak, tight-lipped smile. "I have a few questions to ask you. Please answer them honestly, I beg you."

The pit of her stomach felt strange and fluttery at his intensity. "Yes."

"Do you love me?"

"Yes, with my entire heart."

"Is it a love worth fighting for, worth defying expectations for, to live a life of happiness not according to what others want, but what we desire?"

Her heart pounded. "James…"

"Is it Poppy? Do you love me with the same desperate ache that I love you with? We have endured many sorrows, both of us. We have lost many people that we loved. You have had a hard life with little joy. But I believe in each other's arms we found something…something wonderful. Do you agree?" There was almost an imperceptible note of pleading in his voice.

A sob tore from her, and she took a step closer to him. "Yes."

"I am not a wealthy earl, and when that is revealed, we might lose some friends, and I might have to work for the rest of my life to put food on our table. But I know my life will be grand just from having you in it. Marry me. I promise to work hard and treasure you all my life. I promise to shelter you from the scandal and gossip mongers. I promise to love you always."

She felt a warm glow flow through her body. "Oh, James." The shadows that had lingered across her heart for the whole night vanished. "I am not afraid of working. I will give piano lessons…I…." Her voice broke off in mid-sentence.

"Poppy…are you agreeing to marry me?"

"Yes, I am happy to stay by your side and fight for our happiness, James."

"Thank Christ."

He took a step closer. "I wish I could haul you into my arms, but we are in the middle of the street."

A laugh hiccupped from her. "James, why are you so bruised? Please do not keep it from me. I have no delicate sensibilities to startle!"

"I was in Worsley's fighting pits last night."

"Good heavens!"

"I won." He pulled from his pocket an envelope. "This is a bank draft for fifteen thousand pounds. It will be yours if you choose not to stay. You can live a good life with this money."

"I am staying, James."

He breathed deeply, and a look of implacable determination settled on his face. "I must tell you I am going to return tonight. And the next night after until I have repaid Mr. Winters's money in the month he demanded."

The shock of his revelation caused words to wedge in her throat. He had done this. For her. For their future. And she had been about to run away with the stupid thought that this was how she could save him. One did not give up on love. One fought for love because love endured everything. A hot tear rolled down her cheek. "I will be there, in disguise, of course, watching you and cheering you on if it is allowed."

It was his turn to falter. "Poppy…"

"If this is what you must do, I will be by your side as you do it. I will not hide from it, no matter how hard it is."

"I might get beat up a lot," he muttered, tugging at his cravat.

A teary laugh slipped from her. "I will tend to every wound afterward." Then uncaring they might be observed, she walked into his embrace and hugged him fiercely. "I love you, James, so very much."

A carriage rattling by slowed, and the curtains were pushed aside, and three faces shamelessly peered out.

Poppy ignored them and the knowledge that they would set the gossiping tongues wagging. James placed a tender kiss upon her forehead. "I love you, Poppy, more than you'll ever know."

James then guided her to the carriage that would return her to Daphne's home, made a courtly bow, and walked away.

"I do know, James, I know."

Poppy lowered the carriage curtain as it set into motion, taking her to a future she had not seen this morning but one she embraced wholeheartedly.

Eight weeks later…

Poppy was the Countess of Kingsley, and her husband had somehow obtained the title of a bare-knuckle king, a title only a few gentlemen of society had the honor of holding. They had married by special license only after he confessed the depth of his love and what they must do to be with each other. Life then had been filled with peculiarities but with many joys. Poppy had not seen her stepmother or Lavinia since her wedding, and Rebecca had secretly eloped with Mr. Langston only a few days after Poppy married James. Poppy had received a letter from Rebecca claiming she was on her honeymoon, and from the tone of her letter, her sister seemed blissfully happy with her young gentleman. Poppy had replied to Rebecca, expressing that she would have her full support whenever she returned to London.

Poppy dabbed a cloth soaked with whisky over a cut above his eyebrow and placed a tender kiss there. "I am very glad that was your last fight," she whispered. "While you are a great fighter, it has been hard watching you fight."

"I know, my love," he murmured, hugging her close to him. "We have paid back Winters and have set aside a good amount of funds to help in the restoration of our estates. With the many investments I have made, we shall be well; I promise it."

"I know," she said with a soft smile. Though she had watched every one of them, there were nights Poppy sat in the audience, tears coursing down her cheeks at the painful and desperate lengths James traversed to protect his family and to repay Henry's debt.

She was not sure if this was the time to tell him. They were in Worsley's club in a private room on the third floor. Poppy lifted her hand to her head and removed the veil. Her love looked up at her.

"What is it?" he gruffly asked, searching her expression.

"Are we still leaving on a honeymoon?"

"Yes. We will spend three months away. We deserve this."

Poppy took a breath. "I…I am with child."

A flash of joy shone in his eyes, and his happy laugh rippled through her. "Are you certain of it?"

"I am almost ninety percent sure. The doctor will be coming by to confirm it."

They stared at each other, then chuckled together. "I cannot believe how unbelievably happy I am," Poppy said, emotions tightening her throat.

"Believe it," he murmured before pulling her into his arms and kissing her endlessly.

Thank you for reading **My One and Only Earl**!

I hope you enjoyed the journey to happy ever after for James & Poppy. **Reviews are Gold to Authors,** for they are a very important part of reaching readers, and I do hope you will consider leaving an honest review on Amazon adding to my rainbow. It does not have to be lengthy, a simple sentence or two will do. Just know that I will appreciate your efforts sincerely.

Grab a Copy!

If you loved that sneak peek at Viscount Worsley, he has his own book—Sins of Viscount Worsley, and if you've not read it, you can grab a copy here!

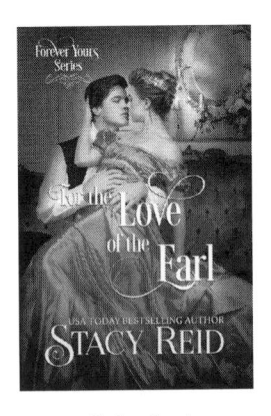

Grab a Copy!

Lord Kentwood, the author of the very scandalous book *A Guide to Passionate Romps between a Lord and his Lady*, has his own story—For the Love of the Earl, and an unexpected surprise. You can grab your copy here! Please note this book was previously published as An Unconventional Affair.

FREE OFFER

SIGN UP TO MY NEWSLETTER TO CLAIM YOUR FREE BOOK!

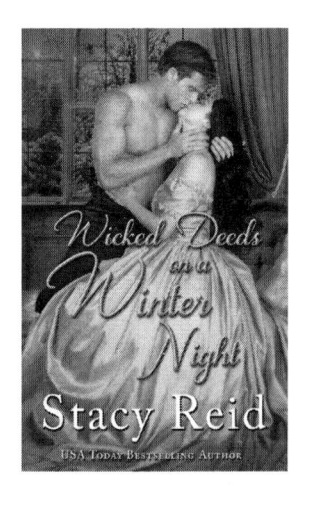

To claim your FREE copy of Wicked Deeds on a Winter Night, a delightful and sensual romp to indulge in your reading addiction, please click here.

Once you've signed up, you'll be among the first to hear about my new releases, read excerpts you won't find anywhere else, and patriciate in subscriber's only giveaways and contest. I send out on dits once a month and on super special occasion I might send twice, and please know you can unsubscribe whenever we no longer zing.

Happy reading!
Stacy Reid

ACKNOWLEDGMENTS

I thank God every day for my family, friends, and my writing. A special thank you to my husband. I love you so hard! Without your encouragement and steadfast support I would not be living my dream of being an author. You encourage me to dream and are always steadfast in your wonderful support. You read all my drafts, offer such amazing insight and encouragement. Thank you for designing my fabulous cover! Thank you for reminding me I am a warrior when I wanted to give up on so many things.

Thank you, Giselle Marks for being so wonderful and supportive always. You are a great critique partner and friend. Readers, thank you for giving me a chance and reading my book! I hope you enjoyed and would consider leaving a review. Thank you!

ABOUT STACY

USA Today Bestselling author Stacy Reid writes sensual Historical and Paranormal Romances and is the published author of over twenty books. Her debut novella The Duke's Shotgun Wedding was a 2015 HOLT Award of Merit recipient in the Romance Novella category, and her bestselling Wedded by Scandal series is recommended as Top picks at Night Owl Reviews, Fresh Fiction Reviews, and The Romance Reviews.

Stacy lives a lot in the worlds she creates and actively speaks to her characters (aloud). She has a warrior way "Never give up on dreams!" When she's not writing, Stacy spends a copious amount of time binge-watching series like The Walking Dead, Altered Carbon, Rise of the Phoenixes, Ten Miles of Peach Blossom, and playing video games with her love. She also has a weakness for ice cream and will have it as her main course.

Stacy is represented by Jill Marshall at Marsal Lyon Literary Agency.

She is always happy to hear from readers and would love to connect with you via my Website, Facebook, and Twitter. To be the first to hear about her new releases, get cover reveals, and excerpts you won't find anywhere else, sign up for her newsletter, or join her over at Historical Hellions, her fan group!

Made in the USA
Monee, IL
23 May 2021